NCIS Agent
Jerzy Shore

NCIS Agent
Jerzy Shore

George Vercessi

Also by George Vercessi

We the People

SEAL~Test

Alma's World

King of the Hill

FREDO: A Christmas Tale

To my wife Barbara

Disclaimer

The characters and events depicted in this story are entirely fictional. Any resemblance to actual persons, living or dead is purely coincidental.

2:00 A.M. Thanksgiving weekend
United States Naval Academy
Annapolis, Maryland

His chest swelling with pride, a wide conspiratorial grin across his face, plebe Jeff Resnick jogged confidently up the twisting staircase of Mahan Hall, his prized bundle tucked firmly beneath his arm. Spurred on by having been chosen from among twelve hundred of his classmates for this mission, he had slipped unseen from Bancroft Hall and sprinted across the yard. Now, all that remained was to secure the GO NAVY, BEAT ARMY banner to the clock tower and return undetected, a simple task, he'd been told, particularly when compared to those intrepid midshipmen in years past who had carried banners to the highest point of the yard, the chapel dome.

Now, stepping onto the narrow balcony, he peered over the low balustrade to the marble landing some seventy feet below and, feeling the first twinge of doubt, flattened his back to the wall. Stretching out from the tower, the usually-active campus, now inhabited by ghostly monuments, lay eerily still. Looking to his right, beyond the gate sentry, his gaze followed the town's low roofline to the floodlit historic statehouse cupola. As his breathing eased he noticed the rhythmic clang of halyards slapping against yawl masts at the Sailing Center, where the school's boats rocked at their moorings. It was a peaceful setting, but not one to linger over if he was to avoid the string of demerits that would surely keep him marching through spring break if discovered by the duty officer.

"Okay," he uttered, stealing a second glance at the landing below, "enough skylarking." Taking a fortified breath, he knelt and quickly secured one end of the hand-lettered banner. Trying not to look down, he unfurled it and scurried to the opposite corner, allowing it to drop along the face of the tower. His confidence returning, he was tying off the remaining end when a sudden gust grabbed the sheet, yanking the cord from his grip. Anchored by one end, the banner flew up and out, snapping with a force to be heard across the yard.

"Damn!" he grumbled scrambling to retrieve it before it tore loose. Mindful of the height, he ripped off his reefer and, squeezing his arm through the balusters, clawed at the errant sheet while it swirled beyond his grasp. Fearing the clamor would attract the duty officer, he swung his leg over the railing and leaned out. In the next instant the sheet was floating above him, and then it dropped.

Resnick gave out a muffled cry as he went over, the cloth twisting around his neck. In the stillness, his body swung across the clock face before tumbling to the landing below.

Some twenty years later.

ONE

Slow and steady wins the race is how I see it, which is why I prefer unraveling the cold cases my colleagues shun. They say it's mind-numbing detective work, akin to pushing a boulder uphill. But I like setting my own tempo, free of outside meddling. Unfortunately, all that was about to change.

Having wrapped up my latest case—an unsolved eight-year-old homicide—I was doing routine housekeeping, organizing files and depositions should the case go to trial, when Jack Maher called out.

"Way to go, Iceman!"

Jack's an outgoing agent who works high-profile homicide, espionage rings and drug busts, which has him juggling several cases at once. If you were to compare us, you'd see him as a sleek racehorse—chasing leads before they grow cold—and me, the slow, sure-footed plow horse. The difference draws some good-natured ribbing at year's end when our cases are tallied.

"You did good. Saw your report, and it's a slam dunk," he said with a thumbs-up meant to dispel any doubts I might have about securing a guilty verdict. "That bum's going away for a long time."

I thanked him and, pointing to the cold case creed above my desk—*Never, never, never give up!*—said, "Chalk up another one for the victims."

In one sense, this case was no different than the others. I had done everything by the book, being careful to ensure there was no duress to negate the killer's confession; at least nothing his lawyers might cite should he opt for a trial rather than plead out. I'm always amazed at what can be achieved once you're into a man's head.

It was Jack Maher who dubbed me Iceman soon after I moved over to cold cases, an appellation I enjoy more than my own witless name, bestowed on me by addlebrained parents who rarely drew a sober breath, which no doubt explains why they thought it cute to brand a kid growing up in Bayonne, New Jersey, *Jerzy* Shore. No matter the reason, it made schoolyard life miserable, where, like that kid in the Johnny Cash song, *A Boy Named Sue*, I was either fleeing or fighting. I could understand naming my sister Dinah, which she quickly altered to Dee when the teasing began, but tagging me Jerzy was downright unforgiveable. It wasn't until years later, while following a lead in Butte, Montana, when I encountered a grizzled westerner named Seymour Knee, that I realized it could have been worse. Then, too, there was the pretty gal in Seattle with a nervous tic—Janet Beane. A nice enough name, I thought, until learning she preferred it to Lyma, the one her Haight-Ashbury parents had chosen.

Happy for Maher's interruption, I noted the time and, unrolling my shirt sleeves, decided to finish the job tomorrow. Setting the files aside, I gathered Sis's financial statements, the ones I let accumulate these past several weeks, and shoved them into my briefcase. From all accounts, Sis was in no danger of going broke, and neither was the nursing home, judging from the checks I'd been writing.

According to my *feng shui* texts, a neat office is vital to maintaining positive *chi*, as vital as the proper placement of furniture, which I dutifully accomplished several months ago by moving my desk away from the window and relocating the file cabinets and chairs. To my amazement, the change was immediate. Encouraged by the new energy level, I set out several pieces of quartz at intervals around the office as directed by the book's author, along with a soapstone carving of a three-legged frog acquired on E-Bay on the corner of my desk. For good measure, I placed a Boston fern on a file cabinet to clean the air.

The only part of my office untouched was my I-love-me display of Navy plaques and ball caps, and police uniform patches. Though modest compared with others around headquarters, it let visitors know at a glance where I'd been these past twenty-two years. Among them, was my latest and proudest acquisition, a personalized Virginia license plate lettered ICEMAN, presented to me by Norfolk's police chief and a department citation praising me for my work on this last case.

No one had one like it, not even the hot case agents, with whom, as noted, I had no interest in trading places. I had found my niche in the cold case squad, which was far less enervating than my previous tour running down spouse and child abusers. Those were nights I rarely slept; haunted by images of wives with grotesque bruises and children with broken bones and empty stares. Three years in hell, which was a year more than most agents tolerated before transferring out. Three years seared in my memory, in which I began each day reciting Friedrich Nietzsche's warning as a prayer. *Whoever fights monsters should see to it that in the process he does not become a monster.*

Thankfully, those dark thoughts were broken when Theo, our resident forensic expert and key player in every loss-of-life investigation, homicide or otherwise, stopped by.

"What's this case bring you up to, Iceman," he teased from the doorway, a wide grin across his bony face, "one and a half wins for the year?"

I laughed. Wherever Theo goes his contagious smile brightens the room—amazingly, even gruesome crime scenes. There wasn't a malicious bone in his rail-thin body, which he regularly abused by entering eating contests, none of which he's won; his latest, a New York pizza gorging competition that earned him a tee shirt after downing nineteen slices in ten minutes, placing him far behind the forty-one slices inhaled by the winner, a feat Theo hopes to match one day.

"That the latest one?" he asked, nodding at the mound of evidence that led me to the a sailor who had crushed a young prostitute's skull after a night of binge drinking, then dumped her body in the pine forests south of the Little Creek Amphibious Base in Norfolk.

"I'd hoped it would've brought some closure to the girl's family," I said, "but they didn't seem to care. They only wanted to know if they were entitled to government compensation. I guess that's what happens after eight years."

Theo shrugged, and offered a bit of wisdom. "Everyone can master a grief, but he that has it. It's Shakespeare," he explained when I didn't respond. "Been itching to quote it. Makes me sound intellectual, don't you think?"

I shook my head. With an IQ through the roof, brains were the least of Theo's concerns. "Definitely," I agreed.

"So what's next for you?" he asked.

"I'll tell you what's next," a voice bellowed from the hall. John Scully, Assistant Director for Criminal Investigations, rarely made an appearance in our distant corner of the building. Rather, he preferred summoning us via intercom, always in the same flat, uncompromising tone. "Come on up."

I knew he wasn't here to congratulate me. He had done that earlier. Scully out of his office and standing there peering over Theo was a bad omen. And while he rarely smiled, his troubled expression suggested this wasn't business as usual.

"What's up, Chief" I asked, as Theo slipped away but not out of earshot.

"Follow me," he said, and then he was gone.

Peering back in, Theo frowned and whispered, "Looks bad."

"No rest for the weary."

"I'll be waiting," he said shuffling back to his cramped office, made more so by Leroy, a fully clothed life-size mannequin spattered with fake blood to demonstrate bloodstain patterns.

I found Scully's door open and walked in, closing it behind me. He was at his desk tapping a number two pencil against a thin folder, no doubt the source of his concern and soon to be mine.

"Read this," he said, sliding the folder across to me.

I picked it up and moved to a chair, instantly aware of the negative chi swirling around me. Though his office was uncluttered, his furniture placement was all wrong. The desk was set squarely opposite the door, allowing an unobstructed path for the chi to enter and hit him on its way to the window directly behind him. Correcting it was simple, just move the desk to one side and arrange the chairs accordingly, then add a wall mirror and a fern or two, and he'd be smiling. I had made these suggestions on other occasions, but being the victim of an unyielding mind, Scully told me exactly what I could do with my positive chi force.

Feeling my energy level receding, I scooted my chair to one side as if seeking better light, and drew a critical look. I didn't care. The improvement was immediate, if not total. Clipped to the right side of the folder was a summary of the accidental death of one Midshipman Jeffery Resnick, and beside it, an undated and unsigned type-written letter on plain bond paper. It and an envelope addressed to the Severna Park, Maryland, residence of Captain and Mrs. Joel Resnick were enclosed in clear plastic. I read without looking up at Scully.

> *Dear Captain & Mrs. Resnick,*
>
> *Your son, Jeff, and I were schoolmates at the Naval Academy. It saddens me to write after these many years, but I cannot suppress information recently learned that puts into question facts surrounding his death.*
>
> *Contrary to what you were told at the time, it appears Jeff may not have been alone when he fell from Mahan Hall. I have learned from credible sources he may have been accompanied by an upperclassman. If true, then Jeff's death might have been prevented. That individual is now a senior officer stationed in the Washington area. If what I learned is accurate, it's time he be held accountable.*

"Captain Resnick gave it to the Superintendent at the school, who, in turn, passed it to the CNO," Scully informed me, referring to the Chief of Naval

Operations. "The boy's father is adamant about going to the papers if we don't do something, and do it quickly."

Unsure why he was showing it to me, I closed the folder and returned it to his desk. "Looks like a job for our resident agent at the academy."

Scully shook his head.

"You mean it's ours?" I said, fearing I was about to lose my planned R and R.

"Not *ours*, Kimo Sabe. *Yours*," he said, suggesting he didn't want it anymore than I did.

"The writer doesn't say the boy was murdered," I quickly pointed out, "just that someone may have been up there with him. Where's the crime?"

Using the eraser end of his pencil, Scully pushed the folder back as if it were toxic. "That's what you're going to find out."

Still unconvinced, I left it untouched, and asked, "What am I going to find out?"

"You can start by finding out if someone was up there with him, as the writer suggests," he said, edging the folder closer. "And if so, you can find out if there was any horseplay, or if he stood by and did nothing when the kid fell. Then," he said, with a final push, sending it to the floor, "you nail the SOB, like you always do."

Again, not *us*, but *me*. I rubbed the knot at the base of my neck and tried a more direct approach. "I got some leave coming," I reminded him.

He shook his head. "Forget it. This takes precedence."

You have to know when not to push back, and so I asked, "Any leads?"

"That's the old NCIS can-do spirit," he said, his face softening a bit, but not the deep lines around his eyes. "The letter was written by early-selectee Captain Carol Rutter, Executive Assistant to 09B." This, I knew, was his way of alerting me that not only did she work for the Director of the Navy Staff, a high-profile job in the office of the Chief of Naval Operations, but that her early promotion indicated she was on the fast track to admiral. "She's either careless, or wants us to find her," he said. "She left a clean set of prints. It's all there in the file. She was two years ahead of the Resnick kid at the academy."

"That's it?"

"What more do you want, the name of the other guy in the tower? You've worked thinner cases. Get on it, and get the sonofabitch before the father goes public."

"Sounds like you're convinced it wasn't an accident."

He shook his head. "All I know is there's a situation that needs resolving before it gets out of hand. If it turns out the kid could've been saved, or, he was pushed, then we nail the guy. If she's mistaken, then case closed. Either way, it's gotta be worked."

It was past quitting time. "Can it wait till morning?"

He let the question linger. Then, with a weary voice, he said, "This one's gonna be a ball buster, Jerzy. I can feel it." Forcing a thin smile, he nodded and said, "Yeah, go on. Tomorrow's fine."

As I stood to leave, I said, "You know, you really should do something about this office, Chief. How about I give you a new floor plan before the bad chi kills you?"

Looking up, his smile fading, he said, "I've been in this office five years and I'm still breathing."

"Maybe it's time for a change."

Holding the same expression, he said, "Do me a favor, Jerzy?"

"Sure," I replied, eager to help. "What?"

"Don't do me any favors."

"Right," I said, and, retrieving the folder, eased out of the office.

Downstairs, Theo called out as I passed his door. "Hey, you look like you just stepped in a pile of doo-doo."

I paused. "You ought to be a detective. The chief just dropped one on me," I said without enthusiasm.

"Tough one, eh?"

"Looks to be."

"That's why he gave it to you," Theo said. "You're the Iceman."

I took that for the compliment it was meant to be and moved on.

I usually begin new cases with a clean desk. And so, disregarding whatever impact the stack of files from the last case might have on my positive chi flow, I shunted them to one side, where they'd be out of the way, and readied myself for this new one. It wasn't orderly, and probably wouldn't affect my chi too badly. That done, I brought out a blank yellow legal pad, set it beside the Resnick folder and, after patting my three-legged frog on the head, reached for the phone and punched in Captain Rutter's number.

"Admiral Cooper's office," came the crisp response. "Master Chief Ross speaking."

I identified myself and asked to speak with Rutter, and was promptly put on hold. NCIS agents rarely get the respect we deserve, especially in Washington, where rear admirals often fetch their own coffee. I was leaning back admiring my ICEMAN license plate when she came on.

"This is Captain Rutter."

"Good afternoon, Captain. I'm calling to make an appointment concerning the letter you wrote regarding midshipman Jeffery Resnick." There was no point dancing around the issue.

I expected she'd be flustered knowing the letter had been traced back to her, but her tone suggested she had nothing to fear from me or my organization. "I'm available tomorrow at eleven forty-five. Will that do?"

"That'll be fine," I replied.

"See you then," she said, and in the next instant I was holding a dead phone.

Come at most folks out of the blue, as I just had, and they usually tense up. I can detect it even over the phone. But not this one. It was as if she expected my call. Sensing I had lost the first round, I began to share Scully's concern.

Two

The morning was warm, prompting me to walk from where I parked at our satellite office in Crystal City rather than take the Metro. I factored in extra time to clear security, now ratcheted up after a recent shooting at the visitors entrance that left the gunman dead and two Pentagon security guards critically injured. Emerging from the South Parking pedestrian tunnel, I skirted the 9/11 memorial, where American Flight 77 was flown into the west wing, and arrived at the visitors entrance seconds before a tour bus began disgorging a load of chattering school kids.

Thanks to Scully calling ahead I wouldn't need an escort and after showing my ID, I was handed a special visitor badge.

Pedestrian traffic on the fourth floor of the Navy wing was thin, where you had no reason being if you didn't have business there. Rutter's office was off the main corridor on the D-ring, in the wedge targeted by the terrorists, which accounted for the high Navy casualties. It was also one ring removed from the coveted outer E-ring, where the top brass—or, the elephants, as some referred to them—dwelled behind thick bulletproof doors that further isolated them. With time to spare, I stopped to view the glass-encased ship models set beneath portraits of former Chiefs of Naval Operations, and then proceeded to the portrait gallery of former Navy Secretaries in the E-ring. Aside from me, no one lingered there, including the two officers coming toward me, who broke off their conversation long enough to eye me, before moving on. With a little imagination I could hear the elephants trumpeting deep within their carpeted offices.

Because of the type of cases I deal in, I tend to interact more with enlisted troops than officers, particularly senior officers of Captain Rutter's rank, but I wasn't going to let that influence me. Since she initiated the case with her letter, I planned to remain passive, a ploy most folks aren't comfortable with, particularly when sitting on what they consider critical information. If that didn't get her talking, I would become more aggressive.

I entered Rutter's office at precisely 11:45, more correctly the outer office to her admiral's suite, where a trim silver-haired master chief with gold hash marks to his elbow looked up without interrupting his phone conversation and, checking my visitor's badge, motioned me to a group of leather-backed chairs beside the admiral's yeoman, a shapely sailor in starched uniform, who barely glanced up from her computer. Set out in perfect rows on the coffee table were several issues of *Navy Times* and *All Hands* magazine. I had just picked up the *Navy Times* when the master chief asked, "May I help you, sir?"

I produced my ID. "Agent Shore to see Captain Rutter," I said without elaboration, since my business with her wasn't his business. Yet, I sensed somehow it was.

His eyes washing over me made me aware my suit needed pressing and my shoes polishing. "I'll tell her you're here," he said, and marched away. A moment later he was back. "The captain will see you."

I followed him down a narrow passage back to a windowless office far smaller than mine, and not at all designed for harmonious chi. But if size was a problem, it didn't seem to register with the captain, who was unlike any naval officer I had ever dealt with. Aside from her age—she looked much too young for her rank, probably late thirties, forty at most—she was stunning—to my mind, a cross between youthful versions of Ashley Judd and Nastassja Kinski, two of my favorite actresses years ago. And while I tried suppressing my reaction, I could see from her expression I had failed.

She rose and closed the file on her desk, a Top Secret folder, and set it aside, anchoring it with a brass paperweight.

"How do you do, Agent Shore," she said coming from behind her desk. She was several inches shorter than me, with dark hair cut in a wedge, and a trim athletic body that had me thinking she may have once trained as a gymnast. She wore plain gold stud earrings, a gold Rolex watch, and her Naval Academy class ring. No wedding ring. And her grip, when we shook hands, was firm and confident.

"Fine, thank you," I replied while sucking in my stomach.

"You haven't had lunch yet, have you?" she asked, stopping me as I moved to the chair before her desk.

"No, I haven't."

"Good. Let's go where we can talk more comfortably." Her jacket was on a hanger behind the door, and she slipped into it with ease. Her multiple rows of ribbons seemed out of place on one so young.

When we reached the outer office, she turned and announced, "Going to lunch, Master Chief."

"Yes, ma'am."

We headed back to the main corridor, the one with the ship models, but rather than proceeding to the center A-ring and the food court on the first floor, she steered me to an unmarked door in the E-ring, and into a private dining room.

"This is the SecNav mess," she informed me.

I had heard of it, knew, too, it was run by the same cadre of Navy stewards who staffed the White House mess, but had no idea where in the building it was, and would never have found it had she not led me to it. The room, illuminated by two brass chandeliers, was thickly carpeted, its windows draped in navy blue and gold fabric. Of the dozen or so evenly spaced tables about a third were occupied. Heads turned briefly as we entered, and again I regretted not paying closer attention to my wardrobe. A jacketed steward greeted us and led us to a corner table away from the other diners, which suited me fine.

She sat across from me, erect and not touching the back of her chair, which made me square my shoulders. "I recommend the crab omelet if you're hungry," she said while the steward delivered two glasses of iced tea. "It's the best in town."

The menu was dated, indicating it changed daily. A nice touch, I thought. And while I was tempted to try the omelet, I followed her lead and ordered the cream of asparagus soup and Waldorf salad. Throughout our meal she had me gushing about past cold cases, including the one I had just wrapped up, about which she knew many of the details. I also mentioned never having married and devoting much of my off-duty time to looking after my ailing sister and her affairs.

Not once did she offer information about the Resnick case, that is, until finally turning the conversation around and asking, "How'd you find me?"

"More to the point, why did you want to be found?" I countered, attempting to regain the high ground.

"And so the duel begins," she replied with a warm smile. "What makes you think that?"

"Captain, I was hoping you'd tell me." And when she didn't respond immediately, I said, "For the record, your fingerprints. You were either careless or you intended leaving them. Which was it?"

She surveyed the few remaining diners across the room, and said, "I wasn't thinking about fingerprints when I wrote the letter. I was interested in putting to rest something that'd been troubling me."

I nodded. Except for the truly evil among us, folks can't suppress the wrongs, either real or perceived, they commit or witness without eventually trying to correct them. It seemed Captain Rutter was no different.

Frowning, she dropped her gaze and said, "Jeff Resnick and I were friends. His death—which we thought was a tragic accident—saddened me terribly."

"And now you think otherwise?"

She studied me for a long moment. "Several years ago, a guy in Jeff's company told me Jeff was supposed to meet someone after lights out, someone who'd get him into Mahan Hall and up to the tower. When I asked who, he said he didn't know, just that it was an upperclassman, and that there'd been scuttlebutt over the years that maybe he did more than show Jeff the way. That he'd gone up there with Jeff."

I hadn't seen any reference in the accident report to a second midshipman, and so I asked, "Did this fellow with whom you spoke mention any of this to the investigating officer?"

She shook her head. "I don't believe so."

"How do I find him?" I asked.

"He's dead. Killed during a training flight in the Med." She saw my doubt and said, "Don't get ahead of me. There's more to this than one dead Navy pilot's suspicions."

"All right."

"Nearly a year ago I was attending a conference in Annapolis. After dinner at the officers' club a few of us headed downstairs to the bar. After a while the waiter came over, and said, 'The gentleman at the bar wants to buy you a round.' We said, 'Sure, provided he joins us.' It turned out he was an alumnus who's a lawyer there in town. He'd been on the Commandant's staff as a company officer while on active duty when I was there, and we started reminiscing about how tough things had been for women mids."

"You were in the first class of women?" I asked.

"No, that was class of eighty. I came later. But it wasn't much different when I went through. There were still institutional biases and residual anger."

"Anger?"

"Sure. Women taking male slots at the academy when there were so few sea billets for women didn't sit well with some folks."

"I suppose it didn't," I said, earning a hard look.

"We did our best to cope," she said, ending that subject. "After a while, Jeff's death came up, and that's when he said he'd heard rumors of a cover-up."

"That's what he said, a cover-up?"

"I don't remember exactly, but that was the gist of it."

"What kind of cover-up?"

"That's what I wondered," she said. "And when I pressed him, he said he'd heard Jeff wasn't alone. That someone had been with him, but the school had squelched it when that person's name came up during the investigation."

"Why would they do that?"

"Because, he said, it would worsen matters."

"How so?"

"By suggesting Jeff's death might've been preventable. That he'd died because of someone's negligence, and how would that reflect on the brigade and the school?"

It sounded fishy, and I didn't attempt to disguise my skepticism. "So you decided to set the record straight with the letter?"

"I wrote it because I've thought about it, and now believe I know who was with Jeff."

That surprised me, and I asked, "Are you suggesting it wasn't an accident, that he may've been pushed?"

"I'm not suggesting anything. That's what you have to find out."

I looked around. Except for a single table with two vice admirals and a civilian in a two-thousand dollar suit, we were alone. The three-star facing me caught my gaze and his expression soured, letting me know my presence wasn't appreciated. No doubt, she would hear about it later. But if she was concerned, it didn't show.

She was looking at her watch. "It's after one and I have a meeting," she said pushing her chair away and standing. Then, just as quickly she withdrew her card from her pocket and said, "Call me tonight, after nine, and we'll finish this."

"Captain, we're just getting started. Who is it you suspect?"

She shook her head. "Not here," she said, lowering her voice

When we reached her office I pressed her again, but all she would say was, "Call me tonight." Then, turning, she stepped inside.

THREE

Back at the office I found one of those irritating yellow memos pasted to my computer screen. *SEE ME ASAP, ADCI*, it shouted. Where would we be without acronyms, I wondered, as I headed upstairs, the distant thunder of stampeding elephants echoing in my ears?

"Is himself in?" I asked Scully's secretary, a wizened sentry who'd been in the job far longer than anyone could recall, certainly longer than the twenty-year service pin she wore like a merit badge.

As a receptionist, she was totally unreceptive. Looking up, she uttered something indecipherable, and nodded.

"I'll take that as a yes," I said.

Stepping past her, I knocked and walked in. "You wanted to see me, Chief?"

Scully's expression was as grim as hers. "Where do we stand?" he asked.

Jeez. Am I going to be reporting in hourly?

"This is a *cold* case," I reminded him.

As a boss, Scully was the best, steadfastly loyal to his troops—running interference for us with senior officers when necessary, and never letting us carry the load alone—truly an endearing trait. If there was heat from above, he took it, which must be happening now, I figured.

"Well?" he said impatiently.

Obviously this wasn't the time to mention bad chi, or suggest moving furniture. Instead, I took a seat and told him of my meeting with Captain Rutter and of her instructions to call her at the office later that night. I also mentioned having ordered the school's investigation from our resident Annapolis agent, concluding with, "I should have it tomorrow," which, judging from what happened next, wasn't soon enough.

In the next instant he was screwing up his face, and I knew what was coming. Ignoring the intercom on his desk, he shouted past me to Miss Personality. "Gertrude, get me agent Ricci, now!" After which, we both fell silent.

A moment later she was on the intercom, her dry voice cracking from non-use. "He's on line one."

Scully was talking before the phone reached his mouth, his tone more tempered, but his manner no less harsh. "I don't want the Resnick investigation tomorrow, Joe. I want it by close of business today. No excuses. Get it here today or don't bother reporting to work tomorrow. Got me?"

Poor Ricci. I hadn't said the matter was urgent when we spoke, and now I could hear him trying to explain the problem.

"I'm not interested in protocol," Scully said. "If the superintendent's got a problem, tell him to call the CNO." Before concluding, he repeated, "Close of business today, Joe." After replacing the phone, he looked at me and said, "I don't care what time you finish with Captain Rutter, call me tonight."

"Aye, aye, sir," I said, and scooted out while I still had my head on my shoulders.

I smiled as I passed Old Sour Puss. "You know, Gert, you might consider moving your desk to the side," I said. "It'll open up the space a bit, and maybe improve things."

She looked up and, parting her scarlet lips as if to speak, shook her head and turned away.

I heard my phone from down the corridor, a steady insistent ring that had to be Ricci blasting me for not forewarning him. Like other senior agents in their comfortable twilight tours, Ricci didn't expect, nor did he appreciate being hassled by headquarters. He had jumped through enough hoops during his long career, and such antics weren't part of the plan at this stage of life. Watching Scully, I knew he hadn't enjoyed leaning on him. Now, ready to apologize for inadvertently setting him up, I picked up the phone and was surprised to hear the high-pitched West African voice of Bernice, the aide who tends to Sis.

"Mr. Shore," she said hurriedly and without introduction, "Ms. Shore needs for you to bring her lightweight nightgowns, shampoo, toothpaste, and strawberry ice cream."

She spoke with the usual urgency, which I could only attribute to cultural differences, since I knew Sis didn't have an immediate need for any of those items. It seemed whenever Bernice had the night shift she'd come up with a short list, which always included strawberry ice cream. I had recognized the ploy from the beginning, since neither of us ate strawberries in any form. We dislike them intensely. It was one of the few things we agreed upon, something to do with a long-forgotten summer in Maine and a visit to a pick-your-own strawberry farm. Still, not wishing to irritate the help, I went along. Lately, Bernice decided Sis preferred hand-packed ice cream to the supermarket variety I had been buying, which meant a circuitous trip via Baskin Robbins. "That brick stuff ain't no good, your sister tol' me," she informed me one day. "She say, it make her choke. Better you bring the other kind."

I made a note of the items, and said, "Okay, Bernice. But I can't stay long. I'm working tonight."

It being Tuesday, the night of the weekly songfest, I was expected to arrive early enough to stake out a spot close to the piano to enable Sis to follow along. She insisted on it. And since I usually stayed throughout the performance, Bernice was free to disappear with her ice cream. But not tonight.

"No problem, Mr. Shore," she replied. "Just don't forget her ice cream and the rest of the stuff."

I checked the time. The day was quickly winding down and my to-do list was growing, but I couldn't leave without the Resnick investigation. Depending on how accommodating the superintendent was, and how well Ricci handled the rush hour traffic, that could be as late as six, possibly seven.

When six thirty passed, I knew I wouldn't be eating dinner. With luck I might squeeze in a quarter-pounder at McDonald's. At seven, I scratched the strawberry ice cream; Bernice would have to do without. It was ten past when Ricci finally stomped in, and, tossing the package on my desk, announced, "Here's your goddamned investigation." Having made his point, he slipped into a chair and said more cordially, "Better warn Scully, the Supe intends having him for breakfast."

I shrugged. No doubt Scully already knew that. And, besides, he could take care of himself.

"I'm now on the admiral's shit list," Ricci moaned. "Not a good way to end a career."

"I thought that was part of our job description, pissing off senior officers."

To his credit, Ricci smiled. "Never ends, does it?" Then, nodding at the packet, he asked, "What gives? You've got Humpty Dumpty and all the king's men at general quarters. Doesn't make sense."

Certain I'd need his help later, I told him most of what I knew, including the part about Resnick threatening to go public if the Navy didn't act fast. Then, stating the obvious, I added, "Everything's a crisis when the elephants get involved."

He nodded. "But that ain't supposed to happen in sleepy Annapolis."

I agreed. What else could I do? Still, I promised, "I'll keep you in the loop as the case progresses."

His sour expression indicated that wasn't necessary, that he preferred staying out of the loop and as far away from my case as possible. But as we both knew, that was no longer an option.

* * *

I was back from the nursing home with barely enough time to go over the Resnick investigation before contacting Captain Rutter. But first there were the fish, nine of them swimming in tight circles near the surface, mouths gawping expectantly as I lifted the lid and sprinkled in flakes of food. Since I couldn't remember feeding them that morning I tossed in an extra helping, thinking, it can't hurt.

Feng shui requires more than rearranging furniture and placing plants around the room. It calls for pets as well—in this case, eight goldfish and one black molly, the precise number and color combination to bring good health, happiness and wealth. And if they died, that was good, too, since it meant they had absorbed my bad luck—a noble gesture on their part. Having replaced six already, I concluded they were performing as intended.

After reading the Resnick investigation, I called Captain Rutter. It was one minute past nine, and I wondered what time she finished work. She answered on the second ring, her voice strong and full of energy.

"You're punctual, Agent Shore. I appreciate that." Then, explaining that she was just leaving, she asked, "If it isn't a problem can we meet at my place, say nine thirty?"

I pushed aside a sudden prurient thought, and replied, "Whatever's convenient."

"Fine," she said, and rattled off her address.

I ran my electric razor over my face, knowing as I splashed on cologne, I wouldn't be doing this if she were a he. I then took the time to choose a tie to go with a freshly pressed blazer.

Traffic was light at that hour, and I made it from my place in South Arlington to Alexandria without a hitch. She lived in the premier section of Old Town, in one of several historic homes overlooking the Potomac River. The house faced east, indicating abundance and happiness if all other aspects within were in order. And while I knew there was a certain cachet to living in this quadrant, it was lost on me after what seemed like an endless quest for a parking space.

"Found it okay," she said greeting me in a lime green workout suit, and without commenting on my being nearly fifteen minutes late.

She was a knockout in and out of uniform, and I had to remind myself to stay focused as she led me into a sparsely furnished living room lacking anything that might provide a glimpse into her personal life; not a single family photo, knick knack or ornament. Also absent were embellishments that tend to soften a room, such as throw pillows, figurines, or doilies.

With its chair rail, dark hardwood floor, and early American furniture, it could easily have been a private gentlemen's club.

And yet, whether purposely, or not, it was all arranged to allow for proper chi flow. The sofa and wing chairs were sited just right, as was the sideboard. Even the gilt-framed antique oval wall mirror was properly positioned. Had I found a kindred soul mate? But the notion was quickly dispelled when she said, "This was a decorator show house when I bought it, so I left things as I found them. I never would've selected the furnishings or, for that matter, the wallpaper or this paint. It's too eclectic and lacks a central theme. Nor am I a big fan of early American."

"Had it long?" I asked, thinking it looked fine.

"Two years. Long enough to personalize it if I had a regular job with regular hours."

Unable to resist, I said, "You should've joined the Air Force."

She caught my meaning and laughed. It was a pleasant trill. "You don't make flag rank working nine to five."

I nodded, and said, "I've heard you have to be willing to eat your young, too." She looked at me without comment, and I sensed I may have gone too far.

We were in the center of the room, neither of us moving toward a chair until she motioned me to the sofa while she retrieved a bottle of wine from the sideboard. Only after pouring out two glasses did she ask, "Is Chardonnay okay?"

I was ready for a drink, and said that would be fine. Our hands touched as I accepted the glass, sending a jolt through me.

"Please," she said, indicating the wedge of brie, crackers and chilled grapes on the table before us.

"Is this your dinner?" I asked.

She shook her head. "I had a salad earlier. It's difficult sleeping after a large meal." She then explained, "I'm usually in bed by ten and up at five." She had settled in a wing chair across from me, curling her feet beneath her. Reaching for a grape, she asked, "So, have you read the Resnick investigation?"

Resnick was off in a distant corner somewhere. My thoughts were on the grape touching her lips. "How do you know I have the report?"

She smiled. "Our office runs the Navy staff, and it's my job to know everything worth knowing. The only surprise my boss tolerates is a birthday party, and sometimes I'm not sure about that." Then, losing her smile, she said, "The Vice CNO and the Superintendent are classmates. No doubt you guessed agent Ricci's confrontation with the Supe produced a few ripples in the pond."

"I don't see Ricci challenging a three-star," I said.

"Well, he didn't back down," she replied.

"I suppose that could be considered confrontational," I conceded. Now, it was my turn. "Does it surprise you that everyone's at general quarters over this old case?"

"Not really. It isn't the type of story that makes the Navy look good should it get out."

We were dueling again. "It isn't much of a story yet."

"I guess that's for you to determine," she reminded me.

"Do you regret initiating it?"

She shook her head. "No, not at all. It was the right thing to do."

"Captain, I'm not questioning your motives."

"It's Carol," she said with a fetching smile.

It's times like this when I crave being a Brad or a Scott, even a Harry. And since Iceman didn't seem appropriate, I swallowed and said, "Jerzy works for me." I waited for her to connect the two names and respond as most women tend to. *Jerzy Shore. What a cute name! Did your Daddy work for National Geographic?*

If she thought it, she kindly withheld it. Instead, she said, "Things have turned a little tense on the E-ring since you ID-ed me, Jerzy. Frankly, I hadn't foreseen that."

I liked the way she said my name, so easy and natural. I wanted to kiss her for it. To be truthful, I had wanted to from the moment she greeted me at the door. Suddenly, I found myself apologizing. "I'm sorry to hear that, but we have to pursue every lead."

"Of course you do. It's your job. It's just that in attempting to set Jeff's death right I discounted the turmoil it's causing. That was sloppy thinking."

"Would you've kept silent had you anticipated it?"

She didn't have to think about that. "No. If there was foul play it deserves to come out. The Navy is big enough to handle it."

I nodded my agreement. "It's come through a lot worse," I said, and for a moment we both fell silent. "Who's this person you suspect?"

She took a small first sip from her glass, while I had already downed half of mine. Then, pushing the tray toward me, she said, "Please eat something. I don't want to be accused of being a bad host."

She was stalling, but I didn't mind. I was enjoying the moment. I sliced into the cheese, smeared some on a cracker and passed it to her. She accepted with a smile, and our hands touched again with the same effect. Sitting there in the quiet of the evening, I sensed I had been invited into a portion of her world few men experienced, and many wished they had. The late hour, coupled with the wine and a river breeze from an unseen open window, wasn't conducive to good detective work. Instead of gleaning information to pass on to Scully, I was studying the arch of her dark eyebrows and curve of her lips.

In the course of telling me about herself I discovered that in addition to being a national merit scholar in high school, she had been a state champion gymnast, and had stayed with it at the academy, where she also joined the fencing team. She said she now jogged three-to-five miles a day to offset the inactivity of her desk job. I learned, too, she had finished among the top of her class at the academy, and had twice been promoted ahead of her peers, at which point the phone rang.

"I'll take it in the other room," she said, and ran upstairs.

I heard a door close and decided to have a quick look around, first checking the dining room—another innocuous space—then the small galley kitchen at the rear of the house. A peek in the refrigerator revealed a rather bland diet of fruit, nuts, raw vegetables, tuna, and a variety of juices. Clearly, the fast track to admiral left little time for cooking.

I was back in my seat when she returned. This time, rather than the chair, she sat beside me on the sofa.

"Tell me how you conduct investigations, and how you're able to uncover evidence after so many years."

It was back to business. Smiling, I answered simply, "It isn't just evidence; though that's important, especially trace evidence, like DNA, which we didn't have access to when some crimes were committed. There's also modern behavioral science, and advanced forensic techniques. But most of what I do is get people to confess."

She pulled her feet up under her again and draped her arm across the back of the sofa, allowing her hand to fall near my shoulder. "Sounds intriguing."

Having her beside me was a major distraction, but I managed to stay on point. "Most of the perps I track down aren't trained killers, or career criminals," I said after gulping my wine. "So it's easy to psyche 'em out.

And when they finally open up, their relief is palpable. They're happy the charade is over, and they can stop living the big lie."

"I don't believe it's that easy," she said in a way that had me thinking she didn't believe I'd succeed with the guy she suspected of being tied to Resnick's death.

"So, who am I looking for?" I asked again, while she reached over and refilled my glass.

She still wasn't ready to tell me, and this time she asked, "What did you learn from the report?"

She was good, I'd give her that. She was going to control our discussion for as long as she could. "Not a great deal. If there was someone else in the tower it didn't make it into the investigation. At this point, everything points to an accident, a tragic, but avoidable accident."

She shook her head, and said, "His name's Ron Espy. Captain Ron Espy." And while there was no joy in her tone, I sensed a hint of satisfaction in her manner.

With that bit of information, I had a million questions. But the one that most concerned me was how well she knew Captain Espy, and if her disclosure was in some way a vendetta. But I quickly dismissed the notion, reasoning only a fool would stir up the elephants to settle a feud. And she did not come across as a fool. Still, I didn't dismiss the notion entirely.

"Have you heard of Force Transformation?" she replied when I asked about him.

I thought a moment. "No."

"I suppose there wouldn't be much reason for you to," she said kindly. "It's the president's initiative. It surfaced less than a year ago. In a nutshell, the goal is to multiply our capabilities by substituting information and high-tech weapons for mass." Noting my blank expression, she went on, clarifying, "Force Transformation evaluates changes in the rules governing the use of military power and then exploits those changes. For example, in Vietnam, our pilots wasted tons of ordnance on such targets as bridges and highways. Twenty years later, in the Persian Gulf War, we had newer weapons, but our tactics hadn't changed. So, we really hadn't progressed much."

As she spoke, I sensed this was a dumbed-down version of a briefing given many times to much more sophisticated audiences. Still, I gave it my full attention.

"The real transformation began in Bosnia, with prototype weapons like the Predator. But it wasn't until Afghanistan that we crossed the threshold."

I nodded, recalling how we had smashed al Qaeda and Taliban insurgents with overhead drones. Interrupting her, I asked, "What's this got to do with Espy?"

"He's the number two in the office of the Director, Force Transformation. Right there in the Pentagon."

"Well," I said, "that should simplify things."

Her smile suggested otherwise.

FOUR

"How'd you come to suspect Espy?" I asked.

"Ron was a first classman, a senior. I was a second classman. We dated when I was a plebe. Yes, I know it was forbidden. When we returned in the fall semester—after summer cruises—things cooled between us." Raising an eyebrow, she said, "If you're thinking this is about evening old scores, it isn't. We simply drifted apart."

"That didn't occur to me," I said, which she didn't seem to buy.

She went on. "After the incident at the O'Club I contacted a few of Ron's pals." And when I asked their names, she replied, "One is a Marine on active duty. The others are civilians."

"How many, and how'd you track 'em down?"

"Three. The Marine was military aide to the Chairman. The others, through the alumni association."

"Chairman?"

"Chairman of the Joint Chiefs of Staff, Admiral Scott Wendell. The others were a phone call away."

"And they told you Espy was in the Mahan tower that night?"

"No, not straight out. But enough to suggest he might've been."

"How so?"

"They said it was his idea that the plebes hang the banner. And since he and Jeff were in the same company it didn't take a genius to figure out the rest."

"That's a big leap," I said. "Why Espy? Why not someone else in the company?"

"Ron's always been a control freak. When he initiates something he usually sees it through to the end."

I was having trouble connecting the dots. "And that's when you wrote the letter?"

"No. I wrote the letter after confronting Ron."

"You spoke to him about this?"

"Not the first time."

"What do you mean, not the first time?"

Noting my confusion, she offered a smile that suggested *you really don't know much about us, do you?* "At my level more work gets done via back channels than up front."

The oblique reference to elephants had me thinking of Scully. It was going to be late when I phoned him. I sipped my wine, and asked, "How'd you handle it?"

"I called on him after he moved into the deputy job. It was all very professional," she added. "We had dinner. Not a date. Just a meeting away from the office. No phones or other distractions."

I nodded, thinking, it may have started that way, but probably didn't end that way.

As if reading my mind, she said, "It was a *quid pro quo* thing. Nothing more." She went on, "We're no different than other old boys' networks. Someone you know gets an important slot, and you establish a link to his boss for your boss. He knew why I was there. And," she quickly pointed out, "if I hadn't called he would've contacted me. It's how the game's played." I must've looked skeptical, because she said, "Power, Jerzy. Getting it and keeping it."

We were inches apart—close enough to discern the green specks in her gray eyes. I was feeling drawn to her, and I didn't doubt for a second she had that effect on most men. Perhaps she felt the same attraction, because suddenly she was up and circling the room as if she had to distance herself to clear her mind. Pausing at the fireplace, she repositioned a set of candlesticks on the mantel that didn't need repositioning.

Reminding myself she operated in a world in which I was an outlander, I asked, "So when did you confront him?"

"It wasn't until our second date—second dinner— that I mentioned Jeff, and what I'd heard at the club. 'Yeah, I heard the same rumor,' he told me, 'and paid it little attention.' And when I asked why, his response chilled me. He said, 'I never cared for the little kike.' "

Thereafter, she had little more to offer other than repeating her belief that he'd sent Resnick on the mission, and either accompanied him or helped him gain access to the tower.

"So all I have to do is get him to confess," I said.

"Exactly," she replied with that same expression, the one suggesting it wouldn't be easy.

As I was leaving, she took my arm at the front door, and said, "I want to help if I can."

We were in the narrow hall, her perfume beckoning me. How easy it would've been to lean in and kiss her. "I'll keep it in mind," I said.

A moment later I was on the sidewalk wondering how I got there.

* * *

I could tell from Scully's dry voice I had awakened him.

"I agreed to work with her," I said right off, getting it out of the way before he was fully awake.

There was a pause, and then, "You think that's a good idea?"

"It can't hurt, Chief," I said feeling sheepish.

He grunted. "Well, be sure to keep me in the loop."

I promised I would, and then proceeded to tell him what I'd learned from the Resnick investigation report—which wasn't much—and of Captain Rutter's assessment of Espy.

There was silence, and I said, "Chief?"

"Still here." Then, in a troubled tone, he said, "I'll check out this transformation task force, see how Espy fits in. Meanwhile, run down that Annapolis lawyer. See if our Captain Rutter read him right."

I was sure she had, but Scully was correct, we had to be certain.

"We're going to need something more than her letter," he said. "The lawyer could be useful."

"I was thinking of tracking down Espy's three class-mates," I told him. "The ones she mentioned."

"That too," he said. "First, let's see where this law-yer takes us. We might want to take it up a notch and have you pay a visit to the former superintendent, the one who oversaw the investigation."

I never knew Scully to be this cautious, but neither had I played in this league before.

"First thing tomorrow call the Resnicks," he said before hanging up. "Go see 'em and let 'em know we're working the case, but not much more," he cautioned. "We don't want to be reading about it in the papers."

* * *

I waited until nine before phoning. Mrs. Resnick answered and immediately put her husband on when I identified myself and explained why I was calling. After a brief discussion, we agreed I could come out at noon to schmooze them (my description, not theirs).

They lived in Severna Park, about ten miles north of Annapolis, in the country club community of Chartwell. Using my GPS, I arrived early and made a quick pass through the neighborhood, driving past landscaped homes with wide lawns abutting the fairway. The few pedestrians I encountered waved, and continued watching me until the road turned.

Resnick's house, a traditional white clapboard colonial on a knoll beneath a canopy of tall oaks, was sited between a glassy pond stretching back through the woods and a modest rambler partially obscured by a cluster of rhododendrons. In all, it was a tranquil scene, and as I made my way up the driveway from my car I could easily imagine young Jeff Resnick casting his fishing line from shore on a lazy summer afternoon.

I had expected the Resnicks to be in their sixties, about the age of parents with a freshman at the academy at the time of the accident, but they were older, possibly twenty years older. Despite their age they looked to be in fine health, especially Mr. Resnick, a trim gent, who reached out and shook my hand with a firm golfer's grip. It was then I noticed the Naval Academy ring.

Once inside, I followed them back to a Florida room, a comfortable area overlooking a stretch of fairway that sloped gently away from the house before taking a dogleg past the woods. The windows were open, letting in a chorus of bird chatter and the sweet smell of fresh cut grass.

On a table beside the patio door were two photos in a folding leather frame, one of the elder Resnick in his starched white choker uniform, the other of their son in his white Cracker Jack uniform which, judging from the boy's shorn head, was taken soon after being sworn in. He was a slender youth with fine features, large dark eyes and a shy smile.

Given the hour, Mrs. Resnick had thoughtfully set out a platter of sandwiches and iced tea. They graciously withheld asking about the case while we ate, preferring instead to tell me about their close-knit community and the pleasures of golf course living.

With the plates cleared, I began by telling them how sorry I was for their loss, which, judging from Mrs. Resnick's teary expression, was still deeply felt. Then, referring to the letter, I said, "I'm sure you know it's receiving the highest attention."

Mr. Resnick nodded. "I expected as much. I'm class of fifty-six. I know how the system works."

And how to work the system, I mused, while he went on about the boy having been their only child, conceived late in their marriage; which explained their advanced age.

When he finished, I said, "I wanted you to know the case has been assigned to me, and what's more, I'm working it full time. There'll be no distractions. We intend to pursue every lead. And, if the allegation that someone accompanied your son to the tower is true, we'll do our best to determine what happened that night." With what little info I had, I was working hard to not mislead them.

"What have you learned so far?" he asked, while his wife sat motionless beside him.

From outside I heard a women's foursome playing through, their voices drifting in with the breeze.

"Only the identity of the letter writer. A Navy captain on active duty in the Pentagon," I said, careful of not disclosing too much. "The individual has already provided a few leads, which I'm in the process of running down. But first, I wanted to introduce myself and tell you how to contact me should you wish to do so. Also, to assure you we'll keep you apprised of our progress," I said, which seemed to satisfy them. "And, to ask if you recall anything. Anything that might help me."

Poor Mrs. Resnick, I thought, watching her struggling to maintain her composure.

"Such as what?" she asked, her voice cracking.

Reaching for her hand, her husband said, "Such as, did Jeff make any enemies? Right, Agent Shore?"

"Yes. Anything along those lines," I said, seeing his wife stiffen at the notion, no doubt wondering how it was possible for a boy in his late teens to have such enemies. I noticed, too, the dark veins protruding on the back of her hands as she twisted her napkin, and wished I was having this conversation with just her husband.

"Try to understand, Becky," he explained. "He's simply doing his job. It's a routine question." Then to me, he said, "We had an understanding—Jeff and I— that he would not complain, no matter how difficult things became. I had not pressured him to go. It was his decision, and he would have to tough it out. If he couldn't, then quitting was to be his decision, too. But he never entertained that thought. He loved the academy. Was very upbeat about being there. And if you can believe it, he even enjoyed plebe summer. Not many mids can say that. No," he assured me, "Jeff was where he wanted to be, and cherished every minute of it."

"Did he mention the hazing?" I asked, recalling Espy's slur.

"I don't know what you've heard, but they've toned that down. Besides, Jeff had an enormous capacity for dealing with adversity, no doubt because of his deep-seated sense of humor. He could take anything they were capable of dishing out," he said, before adding, "as long as there was no malice."

"A rare quality," I said more for the boy's mother, who's posture and distant stare indicated she had tuned us out. "I realize this is difficult, but I was hoping you might show me whatever you have of Jeff's. Specifically, his belongings from the academy."

The request roused her, and blinking me back into focus, she said, "We have all his belongings."

Together, they led me upstairs.

"This is Jeff's room," the boy's father announced.

Jeff's room, I thought sadly. They were still calling it that. I entered expecting to find it as it was the day he died, which is how many parents preserve a missing or dead child's room, but this one had been completely done over. Not a trace of the boy's life remained. The walls, which likely had been covered with posters and pennants and other boyhood memorabilia, were papered with a pastel floral design and otherwise bare. The furniture, too, wasn't boy's furniture. While tasteful, there was nothing a boy would be comfortable with. Beneath the curtained window—a good spot to view the pond—was a Victorian writing table, no doubt replacing a sturdier desk. And where there might've been a stout bookcase with prized trophies and ship models, there was a wicker bookcase with ceramic figurines.

Anticipating my request, they had set out on the foot of the bed a heavy cardboard carton similar to ones my mother had stored her winter drapes in. Resnick stepped forward without comment and carefully removed the lid before returning to his wife, who remained anchored beside the door.

I could easily imagine these two summoning the strength to move on with their lives at some point, and packing away their only child's belongings, while recalling the special place each item had in his life. I could only guess how painful the experience must have been for them. No doubt there were other cartons from his tender years stored in some sacred corner where this had been. Like this one, the others were probably unmarked as well. There would be no need for labels. I felt certain the Resnicks could recite the contents of each container with unfailing accuracy. As I moved to the one summing up their son's brief life as a midshipman, I grieved for them.

They stood stiffly together watching and not offering assistance. I felt their eyes as I carefully removed each object and placed it with the same care on the bed. The first was Jeff's hat, the black brim still bright and shiny. And as I set it down I glimpsed a snapshot inserted in the cracked plastic sleeve inside but paid it no mind. A girlfriend, I assumed. His uniforms, each with his cloth nametag affixed, were neatly folded as if ready for inspection, and I left them that way.

There was a school mug, various souvenirs from plebe summer, programs from football games he'd attended, and one from the Army-Navy game he didn't get to see. And near the bottom, his dog-eared copy of *Reef Points*, the plebe's bible, required to be memorized and regurgitated upon demand. I flipped it open and read the school's mission—*To prepare midshipmen morally, mentally and physically to be professional officers in the Naval Service*—and wondered how often he had shouted that out for some upperclassman.

Jeff had also kept a journal, started days before he entered the academy. The early entries were barely legible. No doubt scrawled at the end of long, exhausting days of physical training and drills aimed at initiating discipline in preparation for the inevitable late August day when the brigade of midshipmen returned en masse, ready to descend like birds of prey upon him and his classmates.

"May I borrow this?" I asked, not wishing to prolong the ordeal. "I'll be sure to return it in the same condition," I assured them.

The question caused Mrs. Resnick's chin to tremble, and her hand to squeeze her husband's arm. "Keep it as long as necessary," he replied.

I thanked them, then, without reason glanced once more at the photo inside the boy's hat. The image was blurred beneath the yellowed plastic and I slipped it out for a closer look. It was Carol. There was no mistaking her. She was kneeling on the bow of one of the school's yawls.

"I'll take this, too," I said, flashing it at them. "It might be useful."

Resnick shrugged. "Sure," he said, "whatever helps."

FIVE

Having seen all there was of young Resnick's mementos, I was ready to leave—to be alone with my thoughts. And so, with the boy's journal tucked beneath my arm, and Carol's photo burning a hole in my pocket, I said my farewells and headed for my car. I had arrived confident and in control, and was now leaving with the unsettled feeling of having stepped through a darkened door. I drove away without looking back and took the first turn beyond the pond, where I found a quiet cul-de-sac and parked with the engine running. My hand trembling, I brought out Carol's photo.

The years had been kind to her. She hadn't gained an ounce or a wrinkle. She even kept her hair in the same wedge cut.

At first glance one might easily assume it was a snapshot taken spontaneously while she secured the bow line at the Sailing Center after a day on the Chesapeake. Like the other midshipman tending the unfurled sail behind her, she wore standard sailing attire—shorts, polo shirt and Docksiders. Apparently someone had called out while she went about the task bent on one knee, and she responded with a hasty smile. Innocent enough, I thought, until I realized she was looking purposely at the camera in a mischievous, inviting way while holding the taut rope between her legs as if inserting it there. It was devilishly staged, and, what's more, it aroused me, as I'm sure it did for whomever it was intended.

Who could that person have been? I wondered. I doubted it was Resnick; more likely Espy. I was pocketing the photo when a dog walker called to me from across the street.

"Lost?" she asked cautiously.

I smiled and replied, "Just getting my bearings." Then, with her still eyeing me, I eased away from the curb and headed for Annapolis and the lawyer who had set this case in motion, stealing quick glances at the photo along the way.

* * *

Tom Ferris's suite of offices were in an historic red brick house off Church Circle, on Duke of Gloucester Street, a short, narrow stretch of road running to the harbor. The polished brass plate beside the door read simply, *Thomas A. Ferris, Attorney-at-Law*. Inside, a young receptionist greeted me with a warm smile.

In contrast to the plain exterior, there was nothing pedestrian about the inside. A quick glance around and I knew the lobbying business was profitable. The reception area, with its polished brass lamps, oriental carpet, and paintings of early sailing ships, held the faint aroma of old tobacco, which grew stronger as I approached Ferris's second floor office, a dark paneled nest swirling with positive chi and dramatic racing photos and mounted half-hull boat models. To one side, beneath a shadowbox containing the Annapolis Yacht Club commodore's pennant, was a glass-fronted trophy case lined with an impressive collection of sailing trophies. Unlike my memento collection, Ferris had turned his entire office into a shrine that conveyed an inviting air of camaraderie in which a clique of pols and fellow lobbyists could lounge comfortably before the fireplace on winter evenings while enjoying good whiskey and fine cigars.

Ferris followed my eyes to a black and white photo of a sailboat listing dangerously to starboard in choppy seas, while its five-man crew leaned hard to port as a counter-balance.

I looked at him, and then at the photo again. "Isn't that you?" I said pointing to a younger, leaner man at the helm.

"You betcha!" he said, coming from around his desk. "But it's the boat, not me, that's the star." Noting my puzzlement, he explained, "That's the *Dorade,* the most famous ocean racing yawl in the world." And when I didn't respond, he said, "She was designed by Olin Stephens." Another blank look had him shouting, "My god, man. He's one of America's premier yacht designers."

"You'll have to forgive me," I said, as he signaled me to a leather armchair.

"If you want to do business in Annapolis, Agent Shore, you'll have to do better than that." Then, moving to the photo, he told me how Stephens came to design and build the Dorade, and of her 1930 inaugural Newport to Bermuda race, and subsequent historical trans-Atlantic race from Newport to Plymouth, England, won handily in sixteen days and fifty-five minutes. He then went on about his good fortune at being chosen to crew in the Swiftsure Race out of Victoria, British Columbia, and what a tough over-nighter it had been. And though it was more than I cared to know, his colorful, swashbuckling narrative captured my interest.

Finally, returning to his desk, he straightened his jacket and said, "So, you want to talk about the Resnick death."

"I do," I replied. "And I appreciate you seeing me on such short notice."

For a moment I thought he might offer me a drink from one of several bottles on the credenza. It was a little early in the day, but I was ready for one. Instead, he said, "I wondered about that, you wanting to talk with me concerning something I know little about."

As a former naval officer, he wasn't legally obliged to see me. Yet, that he agreed to suggested I might learn something.

"This investigation is being driven by the admirals," I began. "The Resnicks have alerted the brass that they won't tolerate it being swept under the rug."

"Which means you've got to show them you're serious about it or they'll go public," he concluded correctly.

"Exactly."

"Okay. That tells me the why. Now, what makes you think I know anything?"

We were moving quickly, and to maintain the momentum I said straight out, "You informed a naval officer that you'd heard of a cover-up when you were on active duty here. That it's likely someone was in the tower with Midshipman Resnick, and the school knew that and squelched it."

He looked puzzled. "I said that?" And when I nodded, he said, "I don't remember. You sure you got the right guy?"

He had the ruddy complexion of a drinker, and I thought another instance of booze over memory. "You were at the O'Club about a year ago, socializing with a few officers," I reminded him. "One, a female captain, very attractive," I added, thinking of the photo.

He shook his head and smiled. "Liquor and women, a sure disaster. Yeah," he conceded, "I remember. You're right, she was a looker." He thought a moment, and said, "I was a company officer when the boy went over the ledge. As I recall, he was up there hanging a GO NAVY banner and fell. A real tragedy. Still, the school was obliged to conduct an investigation. As best as I remember, they covered all the bases. Interviewed those who knew him, including his company officer."

He wasn't telling me anything that wasn't in the report.

"In the end, they concluded it had been an accident. A sad, but preventable accident. He'd gone up there on his own and fell. Unfortunately, he wasn't the only midshipman to die because of carelessness or poor judgment. There have been others over the years. And like this one, most were preventable. Just that previous year, an upperclassman missed the turn behind Nimitz Hall and plunged his new Vette into College Creek. He survived, but not his passenger." He shook his head. "It happens. And, sadly, it will continue."

"But this one may have involved a cover-up," I reminded him.

"Look, I may've had a little too much that night. Probably trying to impress the young lady…"

"You're saying there's no truth to what you told her?"

He considered the question. "What if I say yes? Does this thing go away? Is what I babbled over drinks driving this investigation? 'Cause, if so, you'll have to find something stronger than my memory to go on."

"Mr. Ferris," I said, "it's not going away. The officer you spoke to heard similar comments from others. Yours confirmed what she heard. Now, do you know anything about a cover-up, or don't you?"

He was ready for that drink now. Stepping to the credenza, he selected a bottle and lifted it toward me. "Drink?" I nodded, and he poured a healthy measure of

Scotch into heavy crystal tumblers, no ice. And while I sipped mine, he gulped his then quickly replenished his glass. After that he was ready.

With his cheeks glowing, he settled down and said, "The scuttlebutt among some company officers was that he'd gone there pretty much as a rite of passage."

"Alone?" I asked.

He hesitated. "Some suspected otherwise."

"Did anyone suggest who the other person may've been, or whether he'd been out on the ledge with Resnick?"

He downed his drink, and stared into the glass. Before replying, he went for the bottle again. "You ready?" he asked waving it like a cowbell.

I considered the return drive ahead of me and shook my head with regret, while telling him it was the best Scotch I'd ever had.

He grinned and said, "It's Dalwhinnie Single Highland Malt. Expensive, but worth it." Then, returning to my question, he said, "I honestly don't remember. It's been, what, twenty years? I'm not sure I ever knew."

"And the cover-up?"

He offered a sheepish grin and said, "I dunno. It's possible."

"So, what you told the female officer that night at the club was pretty much hearsay?"

"Yeah," he admitted with a shrug. "I guess you could say that."

I had a few more questions but learned nothing of value. I finished my drink, and decided I would have to purchase a bottle.

* * *

From Ferris's office I drove through town to the academy and parked in the small lot fronting Mahan Hall. With classes in session the yard was quiet, and I stood there several minutes gazing up at the clock tower. It didn't look terribly high, and even less so once I climbed to the landing where they found Resnick. As I craned my neck I tried imagining what he might have been thinking during those early hours of that cold November morning. Bolstered by the optimism of youth, had he felt invincible as he rushed to complete his mission, or had he sensed danger from the onset? And if Espy were there with him, what might have been their last words together?

Every criminal investigative textbook stresses the importance of visiting the crime scene under the same, or as close to the same, circumstances as when the crime was committed, no matter how old the case. Now, viewing that narrow ledge from below, I knew this brief visit didn't qualify. Before long I would have to climb the tower and step outside just as Resnick had; and it wouldn't be in the warm comfort of daylight either. Having become less tolerant of heights over the years, it wasn't something I looked forward to.

* * *

I no sooner had walked into my office than my phone rang. It was Scully sounding weary. "Come on up," he said. "On my way," I replied, but he had already hung up.

It was past quitting time and the secretaries were gone. I knocked and walked in. He looked as tired as he sounded over the phone. I took a chair and automatically slid it to one side, this time without a reaction. Maybe, I thought, he was coming around. Before he could ask, I recounted my experience with the Resnicks.

"So, you think they won't be running to the press any time soon?"

"That shouldn't be a problem," I assured him. "The wife's frail, and I doubt he wants to put her through the ordeal. She put on a good show, but it was an effort. I believe they'll remain quiet as long as we keep them in the loop."

That seemed to satisfy him. "And the lawyer? This Ferris fellow?"

"She read him right," I said referring to Carol. "The guy was trying to impress her with bar talk. And though he was evasive, I'm sure what he told her was true."

"Did he confirm Espy as our man?"

I shook my head. "Claims he doesn't remember."

"You believe him?"

"No."

Scully sighed. "It doesn't matter. We're taking it to the next step."

"You don't sound too enthusiastic."

He said, "Espy holds the nondescript title of principal deputy to the director, but he's no lightweight. He reports directly to the Secretary of Defense when the director's not available.

"This Force Transformation Office has become the tail that wags the dog. Every weapons system, even those on the drawing board, passes through them. And from what I hear, they have sharp knives. They've already taken funding from the Army's self-propelled mobile howitzers and shifted it to satellite and laser-guided bombs. Plus, there's talk of eliminating two Army divisions, and delaying the deployment of several squadrons of Air Force F-22 stealth fighters to pay for counter-terrorism and cyber-warfare projects. My sources also indicate next fiscal year's cuts will be broader and deeper."

"Maybe we should back off until I get something conclusive," I cautioned.

Scully shook his head. "That's not an option."

"Even if it means pissing off the Secretary of Defense?"

Scully nodded. "If Espy's guilty, we nail him." Then, forcing a smile, he asked, "Your passport current?"

And when I asked, "Merry-olde England?" he nodded again.

We had located the Marine, the one who had been chums with Espy at the academy, and who Carol had spoken to. He'd been transferred from the Joint Chiefs of Staff to Commander Naval Forces Europe, in London.

"He's expecting you. You're flying out of Dulles tonight."

"First-class?" And when he snorted, as I knew he would, I asked, "Will you at least spring for a hotel with room service?"

"Don't bother packing. He's meeting you at the airport. You'll have two hours before your return flight."

It was going to be a long day.

* * *

I was nearly home when I spotted the instant photo shop. Ten minutes later, I was walking out with a copy of Carol's photo.

Six

I spotted him as I cleared customs. He was taller and broader than most everyone around him, and looking every inch a Marine, even in civvies. Still, I recognized him by the photo I had pulled from his personnel jacket, which showed him to be Caucasian, but as I drew near I saw he was a light-skinned mulatto. Now that was a term I hadn't thought of since boyhood.

Our eyes met and there was a flash of recognition. No doubt, he also had a photo.

"Welcome to England, Iceman," he said with a wide grin.

I liked him immediately. "Thanks, Colonel," I replied, offering my hand. "You've done your homework."

He laughed. "You've got an excellent reputation in the NCIS community. Our resident agent filled me in. He also said he's sorry he won't be taking you to dinner."

"Tell him, next time," I said, knowing the tightwad wouldn't spring for coffee much less dinner. "Of course he can join me at my place, row twenty-six, seat D. They'll be serving in a few hours. And there's even a movie."

"Your boss wouldn't spring for first-class?" And when I shook my head, he said, "You should've stretched your visit out a day or two. See the sights."

I remembered he was the one who had set the time and place of our meeting, and I shrugged. "Hafta go with the flow. I got a two-hour turnaround."

"Well," he said, leading me from the gate, "I doubt we'll need that much time."

We were heading toward the terminal, and before I could ask where we were going, he stepped ahead of me and ushered me through an unmarked door. "In here," he said leading me into the VIP lounge. "A quiet place to talk without being disturbed." He exchanged nods with the receptionist, and we were admitted without my having to show my boarding pass.

"Shouldn't I have a first-class boarding pass?" I asked.

"Not this time," he replied. "We have an arrange-ment," he said as he led me past a buffet table to a dis-tant corner. "They let us use it for the elephants when they're passing through."

"I'm honored," I said, but he wasn't listening. He was waving over a hostess instead.

"What'll you have?" he asked as she approached.

"Single malt Scotch," I told him, struggling to recall the label in Ferris's office, while figuring what-ever they poured here would be equal to it.

"Any particular label?" he asked.

"I'm trying to remember. I had it once before and it was excellent." I shook my head, "It's silly, but all that comes to mind is Winnie the Pooh," I said with some embarrassment as the waitress stood over us.

"Ah, Dalwhinnie," he exclaimed.

"That's it."

"Good choice," he said, and then, placing the order, he added, "Make mine a Gray Goose martini, straight up, extra olives." And as she walked away, he called, "Both doubles."

I was about to decline, but figured after my long flight, and another ahead of me, I was entitled. Plus, I reasoned, I could sleep it off during the return. Outside, beyond the tinted soundproof windows, Heathrow runway was a kaleidoscope of lights. While inside, settled in our soft leather chairs, the mood was relaxed and subdued.

"So what do you want to know about ol' Ron Espy?" he asked before the girl returned.

I usually conduct such interviews with a note pad or pocket recorder, but I withheld both, thinking I might learn more keeping it informal. So, loosening my tie, I crossed my legs and leaned back. "Why don't you just tell me about him."

He offered a boyish grin. "Can't do that. You ask, and I'll tell."

"Come on, Colonel, I didn't travel six hours to play Twenty Questions."

The grin fell away and, leaning forward, he placed his elbows on his knees and, motioning me to do the same, put us in a huddle inches apart. "Mind if I call you Jerzy?" he said, lowering his voice.

"That's what mother intended."

"I know your background, Jerzy. Know the type of cases you work." He was holding my gaze with an odd intensity. "This isn't a routine cold case you're involved in. I'm not sure you realize it, but you're mucking around in the deep end of the pool, my friend. And, if you don't already know it, there are some big sharks in there with you."

I nodded. "I know about the elephants," I said, preferring that metaphor.

"I'm not talking about the elephants. I'm referring to Ron and his buddies. Believe me, pal, you'd be much safer with the elephants."

"Well, I don't have a choice, do I?"

He drew back and studied me as if measuring me for my casket. Then he shrugged. "So long as you know what you're getting into."

This wasn't the discussion I was hoping for, and once again I wondered just what it was I had gotten myself into. Still, I replied, "That's why they pay me the big bucks."

I guess he liked that, because he laughed and said, "You're okay."

Our drinks arrived along with a heaping bowl of salted macadamias. We both reached for them, and he pushed the bowl my way. "After you," he said. I scooped up a handful and tossed them into my mouth.

He did the same, and together, we looked like a pair of chipmunks.

"What's going on? I thought you two were friends," I said between bites.

"We were. Well, as much as anyone can be Ron's friend. But that was back at the academy. We went our separate ways and haven't really kept in touch over the years, except for class reunions and bumping into one another around the world. That is, until I landed the aide job to the Chairman. Then my old buddy showed up looking to establish a back channel to the Chairman. That had nothing to do with Resnick," he noted.

I understood. Carol had linked up with Espy when reporting to the Navy staff. "Did Espy send Resnick into Mahan Hall?" I asked.

He swallowed some nuts and washed the rest down with a swig from his glass. "I believe so."

"You *believe?*"

"Yeah," he said around another mouthful of nuts.

"You don't know for certain that he did?"

"Right."

"What about the tower? Do you believe he was with him when he fell?" I took a long pull of my drink while he chewed and swallowed. It tasted every bit as smooth as back in Ferris's office.

He nodded. "That's my understanding."

"Did he push him?"

"Don't know."

"Could he have pushed him?" Like it or not, this was turning into Twenty Questions. Not that it mattered. I'd take the info any way I could.

"If you had asked me that question then, I'd have said no."

I sighed. Between the booze and jet lag, I was beginning to feel the strain. "I'm asking now."

He frowned. "Knowing Ron as I do now, I'd say the SOB's capable of it. But would he have killed the plebe...?" He drew a breadth and shrugged. "I don't know."

"What's your gut tell you?"

"I like your style," he said, popping an olive in his mouth. "If I were that plebe, I sure as hell wouldn't want to be up there with him."

"Not any plebe, but *that* plebe? You saying there were bad feelings between them?"

He reached for his glass and, finding it empty, raised his hand and, twirling a finger, signaled for another round. "None the kid was aware of. It was all one-sided."

"Anything to do with Resnick's religion?"

He laughed. "Ron's not prejudiced, I'll give him that. Race or religion isn't a problem with him. He's an equalitarian. He'll step on anyone to get to the top."

"Sounds like you've been there," I said, and swallowed the last of my drink.

He ignored the comment. "I really don't know what he had against the plebe. Just that he didn't like him. Didn't like him a lot."

I wondered if Resnick having Carol's photo had anything to do with it. "You know Espy dated one of the mids," I said.

"Yeah. Carol Rutter," he said without pause. "Who didn't!"

"Who didn't know?" I asked.

"Who didn't date her," he said in a tone suggesting he might've been a rejected suitor.

"Even though it was against regs?"

He laughed. "The mids have a saying. 'You rate what you get away with.' That sort of thing happened often."

Our drinks—doubles, again—arrived with a second bowl of nuts as he was turning in search of the waitress.

"Still, Resnick and the girl were friends," I said, exchanging my empty glass for the new one.

"Carol had lots of friends." Again that sour note.

I sipped my drink, and asked, "Could that have angered Espy?"

He considered it. "Possibly. Ron was very much in love with her. And while he had a short fuse, you couldn't tell with him. It could've been anything. The problem was, once you pissed him off things got ugly fast."

Rather than ask if Carol shared Espy's feelings, I said, "Getting back to the tower. What can you tell me about that night?"

"Well, it was Ron's idea to hang the banner. Originally, it was to be a group effort—we were going to do it together—the four of us. Sneak into Mahan, climb the tower, have a few beers and tie the damn thing off."

"The four of you?"

"Ron, Smitty, Benson and I."

"Larry Smith and Ted Benson?" I said, referring to the others Carol had put me on to, the ones who left the Navy after their mandatory tours.

He had nearly finished his drink and, taking his glass, he knocked back what remained of it and immediately began searching for someone to refill it. "Yeah, it was all set. We had come back to school a day early to attend a party in town. The plan was to do it late that night, after lights out. But Ron changed the plan before leaving the party. He said it wouldn't be wise for us all to go up. Said he'd take care of it himself, and that he'd gotten a plebe to go with him."

Outside, the rate of takeoffs and landings was picking up, while inside, the lounge was filling. I checked the monitor. I had about fifty minutes before boarding.

"You hungry?" he asked, after catching the waitress's eye.

"You go ahead," I said. "I'm still digesting my last meal."

By the time she reached us he'd forgotten about eating. "Hit me again," he said.

I was feeling the booze, but didn't care. And when she asked if I was ready for another, I nodded.

"What happened next?" I asked him.

It took a moment. "Where was I? Oh, yeah. The next day, when we heard about Resnick, Ron comes by and tells us not to say anything to anyone about our plan. When we asked what happened, he said, 'The dumb shit hung himself.' Can you believe that!" The colonel's eyes widened. "Just, 'The dumb shit hung himself.' Nothing more."

I was forming an unpleasant opinion of Captain Ron Espy, while wondering what Carol had seen in him. "What did he say happened?"

"He didn't. And when Smitty asked if he'd been with Resnick, he said it wasn't our concern. That there was sure to be an investigation and it was better if we didn't know anything. That way we wouldn't be lying. We asked what he intended saying if called, and he said he'd keep us out of it."

"Is that all?"

Our drinks arrived and he grabbed his before she could set it down. "He said he'd handle it."

"And that was the end of it?"

He took a gulp and nodded. "Yup. There was an inquiry, but no one called us. As far as we were concerned that was the end of it."

"The end for you. But what about Espy? Wasn't he questioned?" I knew his name wasn't in the report.

He shrugged. "Don't know. We didn't discuss it after that."

I studied him, trying to determine how much of what he was telling me was true.

"What's the problem?" he asked.

"I'm trying to figure out how Espy slipped through the net."

"Easy. No one suspected foul play. If you're looking to find an accident, that's what you find," he said, suggesting that had been reason enough not to pursue the matter further.

"I suppose so. Colonel, have you heard anything over the years suggesting Captain Espy may've been responsible for Resnick's death?"

"Like I said, we haven't seen much of each other."

"Still, you might've heard something."

"No, nothing." He was adamant. Then, shifting to better see his watch in the dim light, he said, "You got anything else for me, Jerzy? 'Cause if not, I gotta hit the road."

I shook my head and reached for my wallet.

"Stow it! It's taken care of. Part of the arrangement." Then, pushing himself up, he brushed the salt from his trousers, and said, "You're welcome to hang around till your plane leaves. Order anything you want. There's no charge."

His words and manner were steady but his face had a glow, causing me to wonder what more I might've learned had he stayed for another round.

I assured him I wouldn't be ordering any more, and offered to buy the next round back in the states, which seemed to please him. We shook hands and he promised to hold me to it. Then, tossing back the last of his drink, he turned and strode out.

As I sat watching the runway, I found myself thinking more about Carol than Espy.

SEVEN

The return flight was anything but restful, causing me to regret having accepted the colonel's hospitality so readily. Unlike the trip over, when I had the entire row to myself, I was now teamed with a young Dutch couple whose enthusiasm at visiting America had them jabbering through the entire flight.

Denied sleep, I tried anesthetizing myself with more liquor, which only worsened what should've been a minor hangover from my earlier bout at Heathrow. Consequently, twenty-four hours sans sleep and more Scotch than I normally consume in a month, I came very close to using the barf bag during our turbulent approach to Dulles.

After loosening my seatbelt and retrieving the bag from the seat pouch in front of me, a move that didn't go unnoticed by my companions, I leaned forward, holding it ready until we touched down. Jouncing along the tarmac for what seemed like an eternity didn't help either, and for the first time my seatmates fell silent as I struggled to keep down the fluids swirling around my stomach. It's mind over matter, I reminded myself while trying to control my gag reflexes and ignore the vile taste creeping into my throat.

Fearing I was losing the battle, I took several deep breaths and, as a final gesture, placed my head between by knees. That's when my Dutch friends, certain I was about to christen them, wisely edged away from me. To our relief the plane finally stopped, and I was out of my seat the instant the Fasten Seat Belt sign was extinguished.

Unencumbered by luggage, and desperately in need of fresh air, I grabbed my jacket from the overhead bin, said a hasty farewell, and elbowed my way to the exit, where the crew, noting my complexion and the unused bag in my hand, wisely granted me clear passage off their aircraft.

The transformation was remarkable once I touched solid ground, and by the time I reached customs I was close to feeling myself again. With nothing to declare, I showed my passport and badge and was passed through in record time. As I approached the exit, I calculated I could easily be back in my office within the hour. But I was mistaken.

Progress came to an abrupt halt the instant I stepped from the huge terminal. The bright sunlight and heavy humidity hit me like a fist to my solar plexus; my vision blurred, my lungs compressed and my knees buckled. With nothing to hold on to, I stumbled back against the wall certain I was having a heart attack. But, of course, I wasn't. And after several disquieting minutes of shallow breathing, I took a personal inventory and concluded I was suffering the effects of dehydration, sleep deprivation, and possibly alcohol poisoning. Moving cautiously, I managed a few wobbly steps, and when my legs didn't fail me, I shielded my eyes and proceeded slowly on leaden feet to the short-term parking lot.

After three failed attempts at inserting my key in the lock, I climbed into my oven, started the engine, and promptly cranked the a/c to maximum. What in hell's name had I done to myself, I thought, pressing my palms into my eyes and leaning against the headrest? I had been acting like a school kid this past week—mooning over a woman I had just met, consuming far more booze than I was accustomed to, and in the process squandering my newly-acquired inner peace. As disturbing as that was, I had more immediate problems to deal with, like becoming physically functional again. Once the car interior cooled and the throbbing behind my eyes receded, I began deep breathing exercises. When I felt my body would react to the commands I gave it, I drove slowly to the exit, where the parking attendant, a cheerful youth, attempted to engage me in idle conversation while I fished for my wallet.

"How ya doin'?" he chimed energetically, setting off the first of two awkward moments.

Jolted by his voice and the blast of hot air, I blurted a gutturally unintelligible sound that had him retreating into his booth, where he watched me fumble with my money as if it were a new experience for me. Finally, extracting the correct amount, and seeing he wasn't going to close the distance between us, I reached out and handed him the bills. After counting them, he raised the barrier, which is when the second incident occurred. When I didn't drive forward as he expected, his eyes flitted nervously between me and the growing line behind me.

"Please," he said, waving me through. "You go now."

But I needed a receipt. And as I struggled to regain my voice, he began shouting. "Go! Go!"

Once I cleared my throat, I said slowly and distinctly, "Receipt, please." This he understood and, nodding, quickly punched one up and passed it to me. As I pulled away I thought I heard him say, "Buenos dias."

Moments later I was on the highway consoled by the image of my fellow passengers waiting at the carousel for their luggage. Admittedly a trivial matter, but at that low point I was grasping for anything positive. Unfortunately, the instant was short-lived. The road curved into the morning sun and my subsiding headache returned with a vengeance. My solution was to flip down the visor and hit the accelerator, not a very smart thing to do considering my impaired reflexes. Fortunately I somehow survived the trip without incident.

On the way to my office, I stopped by Theo's. "Aspirin. Need aspirin," I said.

"You look like you need more than that," he replied, digging a bottle from out of his desk. "Where have you been?"

"Can't talk now," I said, snatching it and rushing for the water fountain.

Next, I headed for the men's room. What I saw in the mirror frightened me—the stubble of a two-day beard, puffy red eyes, and a suit that looked like I slept in it. If only I had. Still, thinking I might pass muster, I plunged my face into a sink of cold water. Then, pressing down my hair and straightening my tie, I headed for Scully's office. His guard dog eyed me, and for a brief moment I thought I detected some genuine concern.

"Is he in?" I asked, my voice cracking.

She nodded and returned to her computer. So much for compassion.

Scully was more sympathetic. "Geez!" he said as I strode in. "You look like shit."

"Always nice to hear an encouraging word from the boss. If I have to do this again I'm going first class. I don't care what the regs say."

"Count on it," he replied, but we both knew he didn't mean it. "What happened to your voice?" But before I could answer, he said, "How `bout some coffee?"

The notion of ingesting one more stimulant set my stomach churning again and, while I suppressed the urge to heave, I drew some comfort in imagining Miss Personality having to deal with it. I shook my head. "I can't be sure which itches more, my teeth or my eyes."

"I hope it was worthwhile."

I dropped into a chair and, ignoring the swirling negative chi and my throbbing head, told him, "If you mean, is Espy our man? Then it was."

The news brightened him. "We got a witness?"

This time I had to disappoint him. "Uh-uh. Just more hearsay. But reliable." I then relayed what I learned about Espy, while omitting the colonel's comments about Carol, reasoning they weren't pertinent. Concluding, I said, "I'll need to talk with Espy's other two classmates. The ones Captain Rutter put us on to."

"We'll have to get by with one for now," Scully said. "Ted Benson. He's in the area. Runs a consulting firm in Bethesda."

"What about Lawrence Smith?" I asked.

He shook his head. "First, let's see how Benson plays out. Smith's on the west coast. Works for the Port of Long Beach." Then, giving me another critical look, he said, "You don't need another trip. Not yet."

"That's what I like about you, Chief. Always looking out for the troops."

"Not really. I'd send you if it weren't for the brass pressing me." Then shaking his head. "Two calls this morning. Both before seven. I haven't felt this much heat since the *Iowa*," he said, referring to the widely publicized battleship explosion that killed forty-seven sailors in a gun turret. I hadn't been around for that one, but I knew of it, of course, and of the heads that rolled in the aftermath.

Knowing when I would be returning from England—but not the shape I'd be in—Scully had gone ahead and contacted Benson while I was drinking my way across the Atlantic. As we sat there, he informed me he had arranged a meeting late that afternoon. "He's expecting you at five."

It was nearly noon, which allowed me barely enough time to clean up and stop by Sis's. This was turning into one bizarre week.

* * *

I arrived at the nursing home as Sis and several residents were finishing an arts and crafts session in the activities room. I waited in the hall for the proctor to tidy up, while Sis broke from the others and wheeled herself to the window overlooking the garden.

"Hey, kiddo," I called as I approached her. "Looking for someone?" I asked, planting a kiss atop her head.

We never really got along, Sis and I. My parents explained it away as simply our age difference, she being several years older, and I accepted that. Later, as I grew older, I understood more clearly. She was by nature a spiteful malcontent, which she later confirmed after college, when she left home for good, making it clear she had little use for any of us. I rarely saw her after that. And it was only after her stroke two years ago that she sought me out. Since she never married—I often wondered who would have her—the task of looking after her fell to me. Unfortunately, she hadn't changed over the years. She was still the same sour person I remembered; only more bitter now for having to rely on me.

Sis turned and looked up without expression, leaving me to guess if I was intruding.

"Sorry I missed you last night. I had to go to England," I said, and watched her eyes widened with alarm. "It was just a few hours," I added. "Got back this morning. I'm working a new case."

She frowned and asked, "Will you go again?" Her voice was clear, but the words came slow, as if fearing I might say yes.

I shook my head. "Not likely."

"Good," she said, returning her gaze to the garden.

"Did you have a nice night?" I asked.

"Joe was here," she said still looking ahead.

"Joe? Joe, who?"

Between the rotating staff and stream of visitors, many of whom stopped and chatted with residents, I assumed Joe was someone's relative or friend. I did it myself, often pausing to engage a lone resident hoping to brighten their day.

Her expression grew tight, and she repeated the name as though I should know him.

I thought a moment. "I'm not sure I remember him. When'd you talk with him?"

"Yesterday," she said with growing impatience.

"Well," I told her, "I'm glad you had company."

On nice days I wheeled her to the flower garden. I didn't ask if she wanted to go, I just did it, figuring the change of venue would be appreciated. But if it was, she never said so. She simply went along without comment. Today, because I needed to beat the rush hour traffic to Benson's office in Bethesda, we skipped the garden and went directly to the flagstone patio overlooking the lawn.

There was no more talk of Joe, but when I left, I asked after him at the reception desk, thinking I might thank him should we meet. But with nothing more than a first name, the young lady was unable to help me. On the way to the car I made a mental note to ask Bernice.

* * *

Ted Benson, or, Theo, as he preferred, was a roundish fellow of peculiar dimensions. His torso, where the bulk of his weight resided, was disproportionately larger than his head and limbs, giving him the appearance of a miniature Macy's Thanksgiving Day parade balloon, or, better, a life-sized inflatable punching doll. The kind that rights itself after being knocked down.

He greeted me warmly and seemed anxious to be of assistance. "So you're investigating the midshipman's death," he began. "I thought that was behind us."

"It was," I said. "But things have a way of coming back."

He shrugged and directed me to a chair. "I guess they do. So where do we begin?" he asked.

Like Ferris, he too wasn't obliged to see me. And so I started by thanking him for doing so before explaining about the letter and the interest among the Navy's brass to clear the case up quickly, before it blossomed into a story the Washington news media would enjoy running with. And, while I knew it was useless to ask, I did so anyway. "I'd appreciate your not discussing our conversation with anyone, for reasons that will become clear in a moment."

He shifted his bulk and the chair creaked beneath him. "Let's hear what you have to say first."

"Fair enough," I replied. "There are rumors circulating that Midshipman Resnick had climbed the tower with a classmate and friend of yours—Ron Espy."

I hadn't anticipated the sudden reaction, and I flinched when he came at me from behind his desk. For a heavy man, he moved fast.

"Stop right there, Shore!" he said hovering over me, his rosy complexion now several shades brighter. "If you're attempting to link that plebe's death to Ron you've come to the wrong man."

"Take it easy, Mr. Benson," I said calmly, "we aren't linking anything to anyone at this point. We're simply attempting to determine what happened that night."

He wasn't interested, and again he cut me off. "You want to find out what happened? Read the goddamn investigation report. Don't come around years later impugning my friend," he said waving a beefy fist in my face.

Obviously, Espy hadn't antagonized all his former classmates, I thought, and I was foolish to assume he had. "I've already read it," I said. "And, to be fair, there's no reference to Ron Espy in it."

He thought about that a moment. Then, retaking his chair, he said, "You're damn straight, and there shouldn't be."

"Still," I said, "there are those who claim your friend was with Resnick the night he fell."

"Oh, yeah. Who?" he challenged.

"I'm not at liberty to say."

He grunted. "How convenient. Sounds like a witch hunt, you ask me."

"It isn't," I assured him. I was expecting him to ask me to leave, and when he didn't I reasoned he was anxious to know what I knew, no doubt so he could pass it on to Espy. Well, I didn't have a problem with that. It wasn't a bad idea under the circumstances. I often lit fires under suspects using the same tactic, and it generally worked to my advantage. "Further," I said, "there are accusations of a cover-up, which might explain why he wasn't named in the report." This last piece was conjecture, but I was on a roll.

He was listening carefully, taking in every detail. That is, until I mentioned learning it had been Espy's plan to hang the banner.

"Who's feeding you that bullshit?" he said cutting me off again, but with less vitriol now.

"One of your classmates."

"That narrows it down to around nine hundred."

"Someone who was included in the original plan."

"Plan? What the hell are you talking about? What original plan?"

"The one that had you all going to Mahan after the party in town that night."

"Ha. I know who," he said squinting at me.

"So you agree there was a plan?"

He wasn't biting. Instead, leaning forward on his elbows as if this were a sales meeting, he said, "Let me tell you about Ron Espy. Ron's a four-oh sailor. Probably one of the sharpest guys *you'll* ever meet."

I didn't care for that, but I let it go.

"As a mid, he excelled across the board—academics, athletics, leadership—the whole nine yards. He was a shoo-in to graduate first in our class. And he would have, if he hadn't spent so much time helping us."Then, to make his point, he said, "He led his class at flight school, and later flew every aircraft in the fleet. Furthermore, he was promoted early for commander *and* captain, making him one of the Navy's youngest air group commanders. Not one of us doubts he'll be first in our class to make flag."

As I listened, I realized I probably should've checked Espy's personnel jacket. But who had time?

"This isn't the kind of guy who goes around pushing pissants like Resnick off a tower. But," he conceded, "he is the type who makes enemies."

"No doubt," I agreed, thinking of the colonel. "Look, I didn't mean to suggest we're looking for someone to appease the Resnicks. That isn't what this is about."

He laughed. "Well, if you are, you targeted the wrong guy."

"Still, if there was foul play, we owe it to the family to uncover it," I said. "And, in the process, I'm obliged to look at everyone connected to the case—even your friend Espy. But looking at him doesn't imply guilt. I'm sure you agree that someone of his stature doesn't need these rumors floating around about him. So the sooner we clear this up, the better."

He considered that and nodded. "I suppose."

Having won that point, I asked again if Espy had initiated the idea of hanging the banner.

Benson shrugged. "Hell, I can't say for sure whose idea it was."

"What about Espy saying he'd found a plebe to go up there with him?" I asked.

Crossing his hands in a T, he said, "Time out. Let's put things in perspective, Agent Shore. It was the week before the Army-Navy game. There were all sorts of high jinks going on around the yard. Skits were performed. Statues were painted. Sheets like the one Resnick carried to the tower were hung everywhere, most from Bancroft Hall. Hell, one company even pushed an aircraft—F-4, I think it was—from across College Creek and parked it in front of the supe's quarters. It was all silly stuff aimed at boosting morale after a pathetic football season. So, if you're expecting me to tell you with certainty whose idea it was to hang a sheet from Mahan, I can't."

"Then I guess Espy didn't tell you to keep quiet after the boy's death? Not to say anything about the prank? And, if questioned, to admit to knowing nothing?"

"You're way off," he said, his jaw tightening again. "That was something we would not do. As mids, we were honor-bound to tell the truth. Anything less would violate the Honor Code."

"I'm a little confused," I said. "If Espy was honor-bound, how is it he broke the rules and dated a midshipman?"

That brought a smile. "There were a few exceptions, and that was one of them."

"I don't get it."

He snickered. "It's simple. Hormones. They can't be controlled. And as long as there were no swollen bellies and both parties were discreet, there was a tacit degree of tolerance."

"You knew the girl Espy dated?" I asked and immediately wished I hadn't.

His laugh this time was more of a sneer. "You mean little-Miss Round-heels? Sure, I knew her. Not in the biblical sense, though I certainly would've liked to."

My hand shot to the photo in my jacket. I hoped we weren't discussing Carol. "Who's that?"

The name came easy. "Carol Rutter, of course. God knows how many of us had wet dreams over her."

"Did Espy share that opinion?"

The question surprised him. "That she was easy? Hell, no. Ron saw only love and roses. God help the fool who suggested anything else."

"Why?"

"You didn't want Ron Espy mad at you. He had a way of settling scores," he said, and suddenly stopped himself.

This was the third person to speak of Espy in such terms. "What might he do?" I pressed him. "Hurt somebody?"

Benson's expression turned hard. "Don't put words in my mouth."

It was clear he had said more than he intended, but I wasn't finished. "What about Midshipman Rutter? Did she feel the same way toward Espy? All love and roses?"

He shrugged. "Ron's a rare breed. Intelligent. Driven. Kinda obsessive. Things are either white or black with him. Not many gals like that in a guy."

I took that to mean the feeling wasn't mutual, and for some odd reason that pleased me. But that wasn't good enough. I wanted him to say it outright. I wanted to hear him say she didn't love him. And when I asked, "What are you implying?" he gave me a curious look. As if to say, *What's this got to do with Resnick's death?*

"I'm saying I don't believe there are many people with Ron's depth of emotions. Certainly Carol wasn't one of them. So, I guess, the answer to your question is, no. I don't believe she felt the same toward him."

We were no longer discussing Espy, and if I wanted to turn it back around I couldn't. "How can you be certain?"

He blinked. Then, folding his hands across his stomach, he cocked his head and said, "How can I be certain? Well, I suppose I could tell you how adept she was at playing men. Or, how easily she tossed them aside," he said, pausing as if measuring my reaction. And when I didn't respond, he said, "There's a term for women like her."

"I know," I said before he could utter it. I didn't need to hear it.

The interview over, I thanked him for his time and suggested he call me if he wished to talk again. Though I doubted he had much more to say.

EIGHT

I wasn't buying the intensity of Benson's outbursts—
they were pure theatrics—nor his two-dimensional
depiction of Espy. Shallow by any definition, the
belabored business about his professional achieve-
ments hadn't revealed much at all about the man or
his personality, leaving me to wonder if it was the best
he could do for his friend. Nor did I buy his twaddle
about school spirit and pranks, or his inability to recall
if indeed there had been a plan.

What I found revealing, though, was the gaffe
about the consequences of crossing Espy, a comment
that did little to advance his argument. And though he
tried downplaying it, it was the one bit of insight that
stood out against all else. So now I had to wonder if
the slip was intentional.

Once back in my car, Espy slipped from my
thoughts and I found myself thinking of Carol again
and her decades-old relationship with him. In a per-
verse way, I was pleased to learn she hadn't felt as he
had about her. More puzzling was why Benson spoke

ill of her. As I sat there studying her photo, I missed seeing him approach.

"Nice photo," he said. "Had one just like it."

I turned with a start and found him grinning as if he caught me doing something wrong, and I foolishly re-acted as though he had. "Where'd you get that?" he asked, waving a stubby finger across my nose.

"Found it among Resnick's belongings," I said feeling my face warm.

"A piece of evidence?" he said, holding his grin.

The bastard was playing me. "Part of the puzzle," I replied.

"Like I said, she was a real lip-smacker."

"So, did you remember something?" I said, pocketing the photo.

"Kinda. I forgot to mention Ron was a White House Fellow."

"And that's relevant because?" I was tired, and Theo Benson and his antics were annoying me.

He leaned on the car and it dipped under his weight. "'Cause, if there was anything like you're suggesting in his background they never would've cleared him. Right?"

"I suppose you'll be telling me he was a Boy Scout, too."

"Better," he said with that irritating smugness. "An Eagle Scout."

"Why am I not surprised? Okay, I'll note it. Anything else?"

"Nope," he replied and stood away from the car.

I said goodbye and swung out of the lot while he stood there, arms crossed and grinning.

Once on Wisconsin Avenue, I joined the rush hour crawl heading to the Beltway. At the first stoplight I stole another glance at Carol's photo, while wondering if he was serious about having one like it, or was that more gamesmanship? A moment later, the driver behind me honked and I drove on.

By the time I reached home I was tense and out of sorts, which I blamed Benson for. But that changed when I stepped into the flow of positive chi. The guys at the office could joke about feng shui, but there was no denying its soothing effects.

My answering machine was beeping and flashing a red 3. I knew at least one call had to be Scully. As it happened, two were. His first message had the intensity of someone running before a herd of elephants. His second was briefer and just as insistent. "Where are you?" he growled. "What did you get out of Benson?" Poor Scully.

Sandwiched between his calls was Carol, asking to call her at home after nine.

It was a little past seven, and my eyes were heavy. I could call Scully or take a power nap. Since I didn't have much to report I headed up to bed.

Anticipating a sound sleep, I set the alarm, turned off my phone, and pulled the covers over my head. But I couldn't settle down, not with the image of Carol on that sailboat seared in my mind and thoughts of Benson lusting for her. After an hour of tossing I went downstairs and sought refuge in a tumbler of Scotch. Pouring two fingers of the amber liquid over ice, I took the glass upstairs and into the shower with me.

As I stepped from the shower I caught my reflection in the mirror and decided a regimen of sit-ups and weightlifting was in order. I also considered touching up the gray around my temples.

* * *

When I reached Scully at home, I told him, "Benson's a one man cheering section. He can't praise our friend Espy enough."

"But is he credible?" he asked.

"I'd give him a six on a scale of ten, Chief. What he says is probably true, but he isn't telling it all." I then repeated what Benson said about Espy's penchant for getting even.

"Interesting, dropping a turd in the punchbowl like that."

"My thought, too. It appeared to be a slip, but I think it was intentional."

"Could someone have put him up to it?"

"I wish I knew. Either way, he's accomplished his purpose." And while Scully chewed on that, I said, "I guess this means I'll be flying to the coast to see what Smith's got to say."

"Relax. You're not going anywhere except to call on Admiral Elroy Poff tomorrow."

"I wondered when we'd get around to the former superintendent."

"The Vice CNO set it up for ten o'clock."

"Now the elephants are telling us who to interview and when."

"That's how it goes," he said, making no attempt to conceal his own frustration. "They want this case wrapped up fast. No foot dragging."

"Foot dragging! What the hell do they think I've been doing?"

"Easy does it," he said, and I immediately felt foolish. He was taking the heat, not me. Still, I didn't like being micromanaged. "I can't figure it out," he went on. "This stampede to the finish line."

"Maybe Resnick swings a lot of weight," I suggested.

"Someone spooked 'em," he said. "Which means we do it their way."

"For the record, I prefer running down my own leads instead of bouncing around like a pinball, interviewing people who seem to be working from a script." And when he didn't respond, I said, "Okay. I feel better now. So where do I find the old geezer?"

"At the Arleigh Burke Pavilion, in McLean," he said, of the retirement home named for the former CNO and war hero. Then, sounding as tired as I felt, he said, "Bring along the investigation report to refresh his memory. I hear it's been slipping lately."

"Wonderful."

Next, I phoned Carol, who sounded pleased to hear from me.

"Hi," she said. "What're you doing?"

"With the investigation?"

"That, too. But actually I was wondering how you spend your evenings. It can't be all work," she said with a playful tone.

"Lately it's been. Your bosses are driving us pretty hard."

"Too hard for me to interest you in a drink?" And when I hesitated, she said, "It's probably not convenient."

"*Au contraire*," I countered before she withdrew the invitation. "I'd enjoy it."

"Twenty minutes okay?"

"Twenty minutes it is," I said. Seconds later I was combing my hair and splashing on cologne.

She greeted me in tailored slacks and a silk blouse that showed a trace of nipples.

"Hope you don't mind," she said, as I followed her, "but I started without you."

"Rough day, uh?"

She shook her head. "Just when you think you're ahead of the curve, there's another crisis."

Whatever the crisis, I was glad it hadn't dampened her spirits. And as I watched her pour my drink, the same label I'd tasted in Ferris' office, I was certain she could handle whatever crisis came her way.

"Here," she said, handing me the glass. "I understand it's your drink of choice." Then noting my reaction, she said, "I told you we don't like surprises. Did you think you could jet around the world without me knowing about it?"

I didn't know whether to be angry or flattered, and settled on the latter. "You also reading my emails?"

She smiled, and I had the strange feeling she was.

We were standing inches apart, the lights dimmed. A passerby glancing in might think we had broken off from a larger group to enjoy a private conversation. I sometimes allow my imagination to run wild like that. It keeps me sane. I sipped my drink. "Delicious."

"We try to please," she said with the same impish grin from the photo. "Shall we sit?"

I took the sofa again while she slid into the armchair. "So how goes the case?" she asked.

"It's progressing. No doubt you know I'm seeing the former supe in the morning." And when she nodded I said, "Is there anything about this investigation you don't know?"

"Jerzy, you're a delightful man, but you're too cynical."

"That mean you didn't invite me here to pump me?"

"I'd be lying if I said no, but that wasn't the only reason."

"Dare I ask the other reason?"

Again that enticing smile as she deflected the question. "Is there anything I can do to assist with the investigation?"

"Can you slow things down for me?"

"What do you mean?"

"It's moving at warp speed."

She looked concerned. "And you feel like you're losing control?"

While I wouldn't admit it, I said, "This isn't how I work."

"I suppose not, but things move much faster in this town. Not like outside the Beltway, where the process slows."

"That's where I usually work, outside the Beltway."

She shrugged and said, "I wish I could help. As long as we're on the subject, have you learned anything?"

Having anticipated the question, I summed up my meetings with Ferris, the colonel, and Benson.

"So, what do you think?" she asked when I finished. "Did he do it?"

I considered the question. "It's difficult to say."

"Why?"

"I didn't get anything substantial from the Resnicks or Ferris, and Benson pretty much cancels out the colonel."

"Perhaps you'll have better luck with the admiral tomorrow."

"I'm due for some," I said.

Her next question surprised me. "What else did Teddy Benson have to say?"

I felt my face warm, but rather than repeat his opinion of her, I told her what he said about crossing Espy and getting on his wrong side. She listened without comment, as if deciding whether I was capable of taking him on, and for an instant I felt impotent.

I gulped my drink, and she asked, "Is that all he said?" And when I hesitated, she reminded me, "I knew Teddy when he was a horny midshipman."

"Sounds like you don't hold him in high regard."

"I expect the feeling's mutual."

"That would be a fair assessment," I said.

"We dated after I stopped seeing Ron." Noting my surprise, she added, "He was thin then."

"So, you've seen him lately?"

"Sure. At football games. Can't miss him."

"I take it the breakup wasn't amicable."

"There was nothing to break up. Just a few dates. I didn't sleep with him, if that's what you're thinking." And when I blinked, she said, "You were, weren't you?"

I avoided the question by retreating into my drink.

"Teddy's got a few problems."

"What kind of problems?" I asked.

"This primitive notion about women in the Navy, for one. Thinks we're only good for one thing." Her manner suggested this was an issue she'd been dealing with over the years, so I decided it would be wise to just listen.

"The service has its share of Neanderthals, men who insist the Navy's not for women. But Teddy took it further." She explained, "He's fourth generation Annapolis. Blue and gold runs through his veins. His older brother was a Firstie in seventy-six when the first class of women arrived. And like some of his classmates he did his best to make life miserable for them. As you might guess, sex played a role."

"Rape?"

"That's a fuzzy area. Let's say there were accusations. For the most part things changed when my class entered. But not for Teddy, who heard his brother's stories and felt obliged to do his part." When I looked questioningly, she said, "Teddy had his own way of working the problem—which is what he called us— and in the process earned himself a reputation he believes I contributed to.

"Midshipman Benson combined rank with his fetish." Noting my puzzlement, she said, "Masturbation. Teddy got his jollies forcing us to watch. It wasn't my idea of a fun night out."

"Nor mine," I said, my anger rising.

That brought a quick smile. "Glad to hear it," she said, retrieving my glass and taking it to the sideboard.

My gaze followed her sway, and when she turned and caught me, her smile implied she wasn't offended.

Having disclosed all she cared to about Benson, she spoke freely about Espy, confirming most of what I had learned. And while she didn't dwell on any one aspect, her assessment coincided neatly with the colonel's.

She also acknowledged Resnick's crush on her, while adding it was common for upperclassmen to mentor plebes, which is how she described their relationship. And when I mentioned the photo in his cap she laughed, explaining that she'd posed for it at her classmates' urging for *The Log*, the midshipmen publication that skewed most everyone in the yard, including faculty and staff. Knowing the boy's feelings, she had given him a copy of the photo.

When she asked again if I believed Espy had anything to do with Resnick's death, I reminded her that I hadn't met him yet.

"What would you need to prove it?" she asked.

"A confession would help." And when she looked doubtful, I said, "I've gotten them before."

She didn't comment. And in the next instant she was looking at her watch and jumping up. "I can't believe the time. You're a bad influence. I'm never up this late on a school night."

"I'll be happy to write you an excuse," I said.

She laughed. "If only it were that simple."

She took my hand and led me to the door, while offering again to help. And while my thoughts were elsewhere, I said, "I haven't forgotten."

In the next moment she was leaning in and kissing me. Actually, it was less a kiss than a hasty brush of her lips against mine. "Good night," she said.

I couldn't help myself, and I returned it with more passion and was pleased when she didn't resist.

"That was nice," she whispered. And when I went in for another, she said, "Good night, Jerzy."

I'm not ashamed to admit the drive home was a blur of lustful thoughts.

NINE

The message was brief, his voice crisp. "This is Captain Ron Espy. We need to talk." That was it, a voicemail leaving no doubt about which of us reported to whom. The order given, it was left to me to make an appointment, and soon. First, though, there was Admiral Poff.

I left my office with Resnick's file, though I doubted I would need it. Large pellets of rain splattered the windshield reducing my visibility as I climbed the west-bound George Washington Parkway toward McLean. Across the river, low clouds shrouded Georgetown University's spires, while down below the churning water ran muddy brown. It had been raining steady since midnight, and if it continued at this rate the Potomac would soon fill with floating detritus from up-river.

The longer parkway route allowed time to think through how last night had ended. After arriving home, I had spent most of it tossing and replaying our brief encounter at the door, attempting to determine if the kiss was a casual gesture or possibly something more, and what I might have done differently if it were. I wondered, too, if she had returned my kiss with too little passion. Now, in the cold light of day I was also forced to consider Benson's comments about her being a flirt—not the term he used—and in doing so my hand went to my jacket, where her photo resided. Reasoning he had a natural bias, I refused to believe it. Equally troubling was the prospect of having stepped over the line. Until last night, I had never done anything like that during an investigation—not even considered it—but I had never met a woman like Carol before. I thought of the booze, wondering if perhaps it had been a factor, then quickly dismissed the notion. I knew exactly what I was doing when I kissed her. By the time I reached Vinson Hall I hadn't resolved a thing and, worse, I had no idea how to behave when next we met.

"Right on time," Poff said, greeting me, his voice dry and raspy. "I appreciate punctuality. Come in." He wore neatly pressed gray trousers, a light blue oxford shirt, navy blue cardigan, and well-polished loafers.

Age hadn't withered his lumberjack physique or his vigorous handshake, but it had worsened the stiff Chaplinesque walk acquired from those untended injuries when his plane went down over North Vietnam, and later exacerbated by malnutrition and a regimen of torture. Sadly, not even the weight he had regained did much to mask them. Here's a man who lives in constant pain, I thought. Yet, behind those dull prisoner-of-war eyes I detected an inextinguishable flame, which had likely carried him through unimaginable horrors. In that brief moment, I was sure Scully had to be mistaken about his random lucid moments.

"Welcome aboard," he said.

I followed him down the narrow hall past a gallery of family photos to a living room with far more furniture than necessary. My feng shui eye told me the space cried out for a good culling, but I withheld my advice.

"Thank you for seeing me on such short notice, Admiral," I said taking the chair he directed me to.

He nodded at the coffee thermos and USS Kitty Hawk mug on the low table between us. "Help yourself. It's hot and strong," he said, while topping off his own mug. There was no sugar or milk, and I knew not to ask for any. In the next instant he was leaning back and taking in the room with a wistful gaze. "A lifetime of memories here," he said of the memorabilia any maritime museum would delight in having, and likely would one day.

My eyes followed his to the wall of colorful ship and squadron plaques and the carved monkey wood naval aviator wings, a familiar keepsake of sailors who made port calls to the Philippines when the Navy had a presence there. I noticed, too, the shadow box containing the grim reminder of his time in captivity, the neatly folded black and white POW/MIA flag.

"What is that?" I asked, pointing to a plaque I didn't recognize.

"My family crest," he replied. "From my mother's side. She was a Carmody." And with a crooked grin, he translated the Gaelic motto. "We do not leap from them. We leap at them."

"I like that," I said.

"I try not to forget it." Then tapping his ship's mug, he said, "I skippered the *Hawk*. Great ship. Great crew. One of the highlights of my career." Then, breaking from his reverie, he asked, "Ever been to sea?"

"Yes, sir, on several cases. The longest was three weeks. A supply ship out of Norfolk. I heloed out and rode her into port."

"I had one of those, too. USS *Zelima* (AF-4). They're the backbone of the Navy. Long on work and short on glory."

I nodded. "I think they invented the 24/7 concept," I said, recalling the grueling underway replenishments I thought would never end.

He gave me an enthusiastic nod, and fell silent.

Watching him gaze into the middle distance, I thought he might be slipping into one of those moments Scully had warned me about.

"Admiral," I said, intending to nudge him, "I'd like to get your thoughts on the Resnick case."

His eyes shifted back to mine without a blink, and he barked, "I know! Cut me some slack."

The unexpected rebuke threw me. "Pardon me, Admiral. I thought you might have other things to do."

In the next instant I was at the wrong end of an I'm-in-charge-here frown, which no doubt had stopped many a junior officer in his tracks, while letting me know he didn't need reminding. After adjusting his gold wire-rimmed glasses, he allowed, "I didn't want this meeting, Agent Shore. Didn't see any need for it. But here we are."

"Yes, sir. Here we are."

"Bit of a comedian."

"No, sir. But I do have a job to do," I said, holding my ground.

He thought about that and his expression softened enough to let me know I could proceed. "So you do," he agreed.

During the next few minutes I told him pretty much what I suspected he already knew, beginning with the anonymous letter that prompted the investigation, and concluding with the possibility Midshipman Resnick's death may not have been an accident.

And though I hadn't mentioned it, he said, "I understand there's a possibility Captain Espy may have been responsible for the plebe's death somehow, is that right?"

I said, "I'd rather not take it that far. Not without first determining if he was in the tower when Resnick fell."

"You read the official JAGMANUAL investigation I convened and was subsequently reviewed by the Staff Judge Advocate?"

"Yes, sir, I did. And there's no mention of Espy. Yet," I said not very delicately, "there are those who suggest that omission may have been intentional."

His face reddened and I imagined him silently counting to ten—maybe twenty, judging from his steely gaze. "That's quite an accusation, young man. Why do you presume I would permit such a thing?"

I shrugged. "I can't begin to guess. One individual with whom I spoke suggested it may've been to minimize the incident in order to avoid a scandal at a time when female midshipmen still drew unwanted news coverage."

Poff rubbed his lantern jaw. Then, pushing himself up, he went to the window and, thrusting his fists into his pockets, stared out at the rain-soaked vista. For a long moment a ticking clock somewhere in the apartment was the only sound, a sound that grew more pronounced as I waited. Finally, turning, he bit his lip and asked, "Ever hear of the Green Bowlers?"

"No, sir," I said, visualizing the ubiquitous plastic derbies I'd seen in the days leading to St. Patrick's Day. "Can't say I have."

Another ponderous silence fell on us while he narrowed his gaze. When he returned to his chair, dropping heavily into it, I knew from his expression whatever was coming wasn't going to be good. Not for him. Not for the school. Likely, not for the Navy, either. And especially not for Espy.

Folding his hands, he began slowly. "There's an inner circle—a cabal, if you will. Not unlike Yale's Skull and Bones—which some say wields immense power. I've been told these men control the careers of officers and thus, the direction of the Navy. How an individual is chosen for membership is unimportant. What is important is once selected that person can do no wrong short of..." Here he faltered, and I sensed he was about to say, *short of killing someone*. Instead, he said, "I am not, nor was I ever a Green Bowler. Nor can I tell you who they are, because I don't know. I know only that they exist, and that they've been around for decades. As far back as the twenties, possibly earlier. I've heard it began with a clique of midshipmen—sons of gentlemen, nothing top flight about them—who took a room in town reached through a series of back alleys, where they could take drinks and cigars in agreeable surroundings. In that room there was a fireplace, and on the mantel above it sat a green bowl. Thereafter, those men and those who followed them selected from six to twelve new members from each incoming class—no more—to carry on the tradition. And as their ranks grew so did their power.

"The Resnick accident occurred not long after I assumed command, and I immediately convened an investigation headed by the Commandant of Midshipmen. The investigating officer's report, which I understand you have, is exactly how I received it. Contrary to what you may've heard or may believe, I made no attempt to alter it. By my reckoning, the facts were simple and straightforward. That is, contrary to regulations, the lad had slipped out of Bancroft Hall after lights out, entered the tower, and in the process of hanging the banner lost his footing and fell to his death. At the time, there was no reason to believe the investigating officer had delivered anything but the facts as she'd learned them. Everything indicated it had been a tragic accident, pure and simple. Sadly, a death that should not have happened."

"But now you think otherwise?" I asked.

He let the question linger before nodding, and for an instant I detected a subtle change. It was fleeting, yet it was there, perhaps prompted by the painful realization he'd been deceived, and thus betrayed. It made me think I may have just gained an ally.

"The following year, the Commandant was promoted to admiral and left after graduation. No more was heard of the accident until that letter popped up and the VCNO phoned asking if I'd meet with you. 'Why now, after so many years?' I inquired. 'Because we think there was a cover-up,' he told me." At that point, Poff conceded that the Commandant, Captain Winthrop Briggs, later Vice Admiral Briggs, may've been a Green Bowler.

"Been?" I said.

"He's dead. Heart attack while on active duty," he said without remorse.

"How could you know he was a Green Bowler?"

"That's unimportant."

"But even if he was, why would that suggest a cover-up?" I asked.

"Now this is conjecture, but there are those who believe Captain Espy is one, too."

I frowned and said, "That might account for what I heard."

"And what was that?"

As a rule, I don't share information outside NCIS unless it helps advance a case. But Poff had been extremely candid and, reasoning he might be helpful later, I told him what I had learned over drinks at Heathrow. "One of Espy's classmates, the one who believes the two men went into the tower together, claims Espy wasn't concerned about the investigation at the time, and that he said if anyone came around asking questions he'd take care of it."

Poff studied his gnarled knuckles, saying more to himself than to me, "It's inconceivable a midshipman would intentionally kill a schoolmate. I can't imagine it. What the hell was going on?" Our eyes met, and he said, "And now I learn Winnie may've been a part of it. I can't express my disappointment."

Jesus, I thought, here's a genuine war hero, a man who lived by the lofty precepts of the academy, took them into battle with him, and survived on them under gruesome conditions, looking as if he just discovered there was no Santa Claus. Pitying him, I looked away and, doing so, glimpsed a portrait of John Paul Jones and the words *Men mean more than guns in the rating of a ship* inscribed beneath it. I looked back at Poff and swallowed hard.

Thereafter, having conceded he had likely been duped, the admiral had little more to offer.

As I stood to leave, he asked, "What's next? Will you be talking with Captain Espy?"

"Funny you should ask. I've been summoned."

His expression indicated he knew what that meant. "Well, if he's guilty I hope you nail him."

"You can be sure of it."

TEN

"Director's office," announced the female. Her voice was crisp and efficient, nothing like Scully's truculent gatekeeper.

"This is Agent Shore," I said. "I'm calling to make an appointment with Captain Espy."

"Agent?"

"Naval Investigative Service." I frequently dropped *Criminal* to avoid erecting barriers.

"May I tell the captain what this is about?"

"Oh, he knows."

There was the slightest pause, in which she decided that wasn't sufficient. "Could you be more specific?"

"Not really." I was enjoying myself.

Another pause, this one a tad longer. Now she asked how long I'd need and was this urgent.

"Yes, it's urgent, and I'm guessing a half hour. Is he available today?"

"Today?" her tone suggested I had to be joking. "I don't think that's possible."

"Tell you what," I said before hanging up. "Just tell the captain I called and that I'm available to see him today."

As expected, she called back moments later informing me coolly, "Captain Espy will see you at four this afternoon."

I confirmed the room number and thanked her. It was close enough to noon to grab a quick bite, and, since I expected to meet Carol after seeing Espy, I decided to swing by Sis's for a brief visit.

No rest for the weary, I thought, pulling into the mid-day traffic. Feeling the crunch of time and the onset of indigestion from the day-old vending machine sandwich I had just downed, I fell into the familiar trap of resenting Sis for never marrying, and forcing me to do what were properly a husband's duties. What began as a minor inconvenience had turned burdensome, particularly at times like these, when I was busy building a case.

By the time I reached the nursing home I had squelched my resentment and was no longer feeling sorry for myself. Thinking only happy thoughts, I parked and strode inside.

As it turned out, it wasn't Sis, but Bernice, who needed stroking. I found her alone changing the bed linen. "Hi," I said. "Where's the lady of the house?"

She kept her back to me, soiled sheets piled on the floor beside her. "Downstairs at therapy," she replied without looking up. "They took her from lunch. Go on down if you care to," she said, gathering the linens and brushing past me, her eyes avoiding mine.

"Thanks. Mind putting this away for later?" I asked, holding out a quart of hand-packed strawberry ice cream.

Bernice was a conscientious worker, but temperamental, and suddenly all was right again. "Sure enough," she said with toothy grin.

If only the rest of life were this simple, I mused. "Who's this Joe whose been visiting?" I asked following her out to the hall.

She tossed the soiled sheets into a laundry cart and frowned. "Don't know no Joe. What's he look like?"

I shrugged. "Sis said he chatted her up day before yesterday. I'd like to thank him if I see him."

"I'll ask around. Lotta new faces. Just this morning they gave me another lady," she said frowning and nodding at the room across the way. "That makes ten. I swear I ain't got two seconds to rub together. They keep throwing work on me it'll be midnight 'fore I get to your sister."

This was Bernice's way of lighting a fire under me, just as her co-workers did with other family members whenever the resident population swelled, as was happening now. Such grousing was intended to prod us into voicing our concerns to the administrator, who, despite vowing to look into matters, was committed to reducing costs by doing more with less.

I nodded. "I'll speak to Mr. West."

"Somebody's got to," she said with a huff.

"Guess I'll go see Sis."

"Yeah. She'll be happy to see you," she said, two-stepping to the refrigerator behind the nurses' station, the linen cart momentarily forgotten.

The therapy clinic downstairs operated with the efficiency of an assembly line, pushing patients through quarter-hour regimens that did little more than break up their otherwise boring days. If there were physical improvements they were difficult to discern. Yet the scene rarely varied; a handful of therapists overseeing patients under the glassy-eyed stares of those awaiting their turn. Amazingly, no one complained. But why should they? They had little else to do. For me, though, it was a depressing spectacle.

I spotted Sis across the room with those who had completed their workouts. Always alert, she was watching the activities as if she had a personal stake in each resident's progress. The director, a swarthy Indian with a cloying manner, saw me from his office and came bouncing over, a wide grin on his face. The guy never missed a chance to schmooze with us check-writers.

"So nice to see you, Mr. Shore," he said in a clipped accent. "Miss Shore is doing very well. We are all very proud of her."

"Glad to hear it," I replied, knowing her condition hadn't improved measurably over the past six months.

Then, leaning down and pressing his face into hers as if she were a moron capable of grasping only the simplest notions, he raised his voice and said, "Aren't you, Miss Shore?" I watched her blink with each word, an awkward placating smile breaking across her face, while understanding fully this was all just a game. "We are seeing wonderful progress. At this rate you'll be going home very soon," he said to her. Then, in case I missed it, he looked to me and repeated, "She'll be going home in no time."

I saw her eyes mist and my stomach knotted. We both knew going home wasn't an option. We had already resolved that decision when I explained that I couldn't provide the level of care she required. Yet she smiled and nodded compliantly, because that's what you do when you're helpless and under the control of strangers.

What made the notion more offensive was knowing Rajeev, or whatever the little sycophant's name was, had no more interest in seeing her discharged than Mr. West, the administrator, another weasel whose annual bonus depended on keeping every bed filled and costs down, and who always managed to find me at month's end when the bill was due to be sure I knew how much she was improving.

"Your sister is finished for today," he said, "but you are welcome to stay if you like, Mr. Shore."

Yeah, right. That's exactly how I want to spend my lunch time, watching invalids in diapers doing leg raises. For Sis's sake, I swallowed my resentment and smiled. "I think we'll go outside," I said. "It's such a beautiful day."

While heading for the elevator, I wondered how much longer they would have left her sitting there.

Probably, I decided with growing resentment, till Bernice came to fetch her for supper.

"So," I asked once we were settled on the patio, "seen Joe lately?"

Her expression brightened and she nodded enthusiastically. "Last night. We had a long chat. He's very nice."

"What'd you talk about?"

She shrugged. "We just talked."

Sis's attention span had diminished since her stroke, so I was never sure when our conversations would end. "When last night?" I asked.

"After dinner." She said it as though I was intruding, and I recalled the times as youngsters when she would shut me out of her life, oftentimes as though I didn't exist.

Still, I tried pinning her down, but she had already shifted her attention to a flock of crows that had swooped onto the lawn and were pecking it clean of insects. After a while, I asked, "Did Joe stay long?" She was off somewhere in her own world and didn't reply. I shook my head. So many of our conversations were one-sided.

Before leaving, I took her back inside and deposited her among several residents sitting quietly in the lobby listening to the radio. I turned and waved, but she didn't respond.

* * *

It was about two when I returned to the office; time enough before meeting Espy to review Resnick's journal. Written thoughtfully, it provided my first insight into the boy, who made it clear that his singular goal in life was gaining entry to the academy and ultimately a naval career. I started with his musings set down the night before reporting in. He wrote not hurriedly, but in a stream of nervous energy that had me imagining him sequestered in his room, alternately writing and gazing at the pond. Filling nearly two pages, he reflected on how pleased he was at making the cut and being accepted. He wondered, too, how his life was about to change, while speculating if his plebe summer would differ much from his father's. It was a moving account that must have devastated his mother when she later found it.

He went on describing his pride that first hectic day when joining a thousand other benumbed classmates in uniform before Bancroft Hall to take the midshipman's oath of office under the anxious eyes of his parents. And though he remained faithful to the task, future entries grew shorter. There were scribbled notes before taps and jottings before breakfast recounting the grinding dawn-to-dusk routine from the point of view of one who welcomed the challenge.

Soon his focus shifted, and he wrote not so much of himself but of his fellow plebes, and I knew the bonding process had begun. By his own admission, they were making great strides and looking forward to Parents

Weekend, when returning families would surely marvel at their transformation from raw recruits to a well-honed military unit.

I noticed, too, as summer drew to a close he grew concerned over persistent rumors, no doubt intentionally spread, about what he and his classmates could expect when the semester began and their core unit would be divvied up among the Brigade's thirty-six companies. And while I recognized it as more psychological pressure from upperclassmen, he clearly did not. Knowing he would soon be leaving the protection of the herd, he confessed to being less confident of coping with the harsh regimen awaiting him. Thereafter there followed dark passages, in which he brooded over the prospect of his lowly status in his assigned company, and what demands his new superiors might place on him.

As I read on, I saw he had been right to worry. September began badly for him and had gotten worse, so that by October he was foregoing sleep to maintain his grades. Shifting to cryptic shorthand, he alluded to stepped-up levels of hazing, and conflicts with upperclassmen who he speculated were singling him out because his father went through earlier. I paged ahead, wondering if one of his tormentors had been Espy but, whether out of misguided loyalty or paranoia, he withheld such details. Regardless, it was clear Resnick wasn't a happy camper. Still, all wasn't harsh. On the positive side, he mentioned new friendships, including his mentorship with Carol. It was a good place to end, and so I closed the journal.

I checked the time. I'd soon be confronting Espy with nothing more than hearsay. By not allowing me to proceed at my own pace, the admirals in the E-ring had advanced my timetable and, like Midshipman Resnick, I was also being distracted by pressure from above.

I had just closed my eyes and was focusing on the positive energy flowing around me when my phone rang. "Lord," I muttered, "give me a break."

It was Scully sounding like a coach before the kick-off. "Hey, Iceman, you ready for Espy?"

"Sure," I said, bracing for additional rudder orders. "Why do you ask?"

"The guy's a heavy hitter."

I was growing tired of his intrusions, and now this implication that I wasn't up to the task sent me over the edge. "We already discussed that," I shot back. "If you don't feel comfortable with me maybe you should send in someone else." The words no sooner left my mouth and I regretted the outburst. Scully didn't deserve it.

"Take it easy," he said. "I'm on your side."

"I know, Chief. It's just that... The way we're proceeding... It's not how I operate, is all." I was mindlessly riffling Resnick's journal pages while Scully sympathized with me.

"I agree. This isn't the way to do business," he was saying when I noticed a slight irregularity between the pages. While he went on about doing what I usually do, I leaned in for a closer look.

"Go in there and make him sweat," he said. "Make him feel the heat." When I didn't respond, he said, "Jerzy, you there?"

Several pages were missing.

"Jerzy!"

"Right here, Chief."

"You listening?"

"Yes, Chief," I said while searching my bottom drawer for a magnifying glass.

"I want you to twist this guy's tail." And when I didn't reply this time he blew a gasket. "What the hell're you doing?"

"Sorry, Chief. I just noticed Resnick diary's missing a few pages. Looks like someone cut them out with a razor."

But he wasn't interested. "Forget the damn diary. I'm talking about your friggin' meeting today."

Scully rarely swore, and since *damn* and *friggin'* was as bad as it usually got I gave him my full attention.

"The clock's running," he said. "It's critical that you come away with something today. Something we can nail him on. I don't care how flimsy, so long as we can use it."

I was tempted to ask, why the rush, but held my silence. Scully had never worked a cold case, so he didn't appreciate the ins and outs of identifying and analyzing old evidence and constructing time lines. He was more accustomed to techniques like the good-cop, bad-cop routine that yield quick results from young, impressionable sailors. And while they could be effective, they tended not to work as well with cold case suspects who had learned to live with their crimes for years, often decades.

"This is beginning to sound like a lynching party, Chief. Care to tell me what's going on?" I don't know why I asked. I knew he wasn't going to tell me.

Unfortunately, that set him off again. "What's going on is you're going to nail that SOB." This wasn't the Scully I knew. He was unraveling, and we both knew it. It had to be the pressure from above.

"Don't worry, Chief," I said, regretting my petulance. "If there's something, I'll get it."

"What's that mean?" he barked.

I bit my tongue. "It means if he's guilty I'll nail him."

"*If* he's guilty?" He wasn't going to yield.

"Chief, we're dealing with a possible homicide," I reminded him. "We got squat for evidence, and nothing that contradicts the official investigation. So, I'm allowing myself some wiggle room."

"Your job's to squeeze him. I'll worry about whether we have a case."

I took a breath and said, "To be honest, Chief, I'm feeling command pressure here." There, I'd said it, and I steeled myself for the next incoming round.

"Don't ever use that term! That's the last friggin' thing anybody wants to hear." If I were in his office I think he would have lunged at me. "There is no command pressure," he insisted. "This case stands or falls on its merits. You got that?"

Of course I got it. I was being pressured, and I had better not be dumb enough to mention it again. Still, I disliked being someone's hand puppet, and so I said, "You sure there isn't something you aren't telling me?" There was silence, and it was my turn to ask, "You still there, Chief?"

"Don't be a smart ass." Then, taking a breath, he said more tolerantly, "The thing is we don't have a lot of time. You understand?"

I wanted to say, "No, I don't understand much of anything." By now even the idea that the Resnicks were putting pressure on the Navy no longer seemed credible. But saying so would only prolong this pointless discussion. So instead, I said, "Sure, Chief," which seemed to mollify him.

"Good. Now let's put this thing to bed."

I hung up craving the big picture and knowing I wasn't going to get it from Scully. I thought of asking Carol. No doubt she knew more of what was driving this beast, but I suspected she wouldn't say much either and, besides, doing an end run around Scully wasn't a good idea.

Meanwhile, there was Resnick's journal. I found the magnifying glass buried in a cigar box in my lower junk drawer. What was it the feng shui books said about clutter? Ah yes, *clutter creates disharmony*. "Can't argue with that," I muttered.

A closer inspection revealed three pages had been neatly removed close to the book's spine with a sharp blade. And since there were no entries after that, I assumed they contained Resnick's final thoughts before he headed to the tower, and probably the name of the person who put him up to it, as well. Why else remove them?

* * *

Espy's office was far removed from the Secretary of Defense's, which surprised me, considering his exalted status. Still, he had the distinction of being in the Pentagon's prime real estate—the prized E-ring.

As I headed in that direction, I noticed folks slowing their pace and lowering their voices, and I realized I had entered the section attacked on 9/11. And while it looked like the other corridors, the walls here were decorated with drawings and posters with images of that fatal day, many by schoolchildren. There were quilts, too, depicting the American flag and other symbols of Americana. Up ahead, a soldier in dress uniform was escorting his tour group into the 9/11 memorial room. I had heard about it, but hadn't seen it and, with time to spare I fell in behind them.

The room itself was small, dark and somber, with the names of those aboard the aircraft listed on one wall, and those killed inside the building displayed on another; 184 in all. Hardly anyone spoke as they moved about; a few were busy making pencil rubbings of individuals who'd perished. A second door led to the memorial garden outside. As the group moved in that direction, I returned to the corridor and headed upstairs to Espy's office.

Unlike neighboring VIP spaces, there were no flags or portraits here, just bare walls and metal doors with magnetic lock boxes. The nameplate was easy to miss; a simple, unassuming card that read *Force Transformation* and the room number below it. Had I passed by the previous week when first calling on Carol, it would have had no meaning. But now I knew it was the president's brainchild, and its goal was to convert our military to a seamless ultra-modern force capable of defeating our enemies with weapons only science fiction writers could envision.

I also learned the plan had its detractors, many of whom were entrenched right there in the Pentagon, Cold War bureaucrats who were wedded to weapons systems that no longer supported this administration's goals.

And while I knew far less about such things than many in this five-sided palace, I understood why the Force Transformation director, a retired vice admiral, and his able assistant, Captain Ronald Espy, kept a low profile. Together, they were using the age-old tactic of divide and conquer—playing the services and their congressional supporters off each other. And as most Washingtonians knew, that was a dangerous game.

I pressed the buzzer beside the door and waited while someone peered at me through the peephole. After a moment the lock clicked and a handsome middle-aged woman cracked the door several inches. "May I help you?" she asked.

I recognized the voice as the woman I had spoken with earlier. Not surprising, she was no friendlier in person.

"Agent Shore to see Captain Espy."

She opened the door a few inches more. "May I see some identification?"

I flipped open my wallet, and was surprised when she focused on my ID rather than my shield, which satisfied most folks, shifting her gaze from the photo to me and back again. It was an old photo, one that downplayed the aging process, which is why I kept it. Who says NCIS agents aren't vain?

"Doesn't look much like you," she noted.

I grinned. "It does after a few drinks."

Ignoring my humor, she stepped aside and allowed me entry into what can only be described as a windowless bowling alley painted a mind-numbing pale green. More a work space than an office, it was minimally furnished with three desks in tandem along one wall, several file cabinets with large tumbler locks, and a worn leather armchair shoved in the corner near the door like an afterthought. Whatever money was being saved in consolidating our weapons systems clearly wasn't being spent here. But then, Espy probably didn't have many visitors.

The first desk, the one nearest the door, was hers. The others were occupied by grim-faced majors, one Army and one Air Force, with Bluetooth headphone sets, who gave me a cursory glance without breaking their phone conversations.

"The captain hasn't returned yet," she said pointing to the chair. "He's running late."

"How long will he be delayed?" I asked, the query drawing snickers from Twiddle Dee and Tweedle Dum.

This woman, who wore little or no makeup, was quick, and, to her credit, not about to be coerced. "He's with the secretary," she said, letting me know my place in the pecking order.

"Right," I said, and settled back to wait.

It didn't take long to figure out they were running a glorified boiler room operation, not unlike those annoying telemarketers who interrupted my dinner before I added my phone number to the National Do Not Call List. I say glorified, because of who they were calling—congressmen and senators, mostly. Well, their staffs, anyway. Stone-faced and working independently, the majors kept a steady pace, never rushing and always courteous, while staying on point with each call as long as necessary.

I passed the time mentally rearranging their bleak corner of the Pentagon, where the only splash of color was a lone yellow rose in a plain glass vase on the woman's desk. Oddly, there were no personal items to be seen. It was as if the occupants were granted use of the space without permission to claim any portion of it. Given the limited space and dimensions, I concluded it would take a feng shui master to bring harmony to it. Still, I tried; envisioning a mirror here, a plant there, a few well-positioned crystals and, of course, a new coat of paint.

I thought of Scully's reception area, with Miss Congeniality's multi-generation family photos and colorful Beanie Babies collection. More than once I'd been tempted to return at night and haul the entire menagerie to the burn room, where we destroyed classified documents. But knowing the hell she'd put poor Scully through the following day, I refrained.

Lacking other distractions, I returned to the yellow rose and the woman, wondering who had presented it to her, and why. Was today her birthday? Not likely. Not without a card. And since she was ringless, I ruled out an anniversary. Oddly, she wore no jewelry, not even a watch. Who doesn't wear a watch? Someone not on a schedule. Someone who arrives early, stays late, and doesn't care what time she gets home. In other words, an unattached workaholic without a pet to feed. I was certain I had her number.

It was only when she went to one of the file cabinets that I noticed her shapely farm girl figure. She had a pleasant face now that she wasn't scowling. Suspecting a little office romance, I watched the majors, expecting a stolen glance as she brushed past them, but they were as oblivious of her as she was of them.

So, if the rose hadn't come from either of them, who then? Captain Espy came to mind, and I quickly dismissed the notion. From what I was learning, he wouldn't date anyone of lesser military or social rank.

I had been waiting nearly an hour when the door finally opened and our hero presented himself. Without acknowledging me, he gathered his ducklings at the far end of the office for an impromptu meeting, where he pumped them for updates on several obscure issues.

As I watched, I wondered if any of this was for my benefit, and decided probably not. In the next moment I was thinking of Carol having dinner with this Navy poster boy. It wasn't a pleasant image, these two hard-charging professionals supping in quiet candlelight before heading back to her place for a drink and whatever. It was the whatever that bothered me most.

I must admit to a touch of jealousy sitting there on the sideline watching him holding court in his tailored uniform, crisp white shirt and gleaming shoes. And when he finally looked my way I sensed he knew what I was thinking. It was a peculiar moment that left me feeling exposed and vulnerable. He turned away just as quickly, and I wondered which of us was the hunter and which the prey.

"For the director," I heard him instruct the woman, handing her a sheaf of files. And in the next breath he summoned me. "Agent Shore."

I nodded and, coming over, I extended my hand, which he ignored.

"Come in," he said, moving ahead of me.

This guy's a master of one-upmanship, I decided, following him inside. But the impression quickly faded when he moved to shut the door and I detected a hint of concern as he looked past me at the two majors watching us. *Got ya, big fella.* This isn't a meeting you wanted, and certainly not here in front of the troops.

Unlike the Spartan ante-room, Espy's office had all the trappings I expected to find in this upscale address—plush carpeting, maroon leather chairs, a broad executive desk and matching conference table, and the coveted view of Arlington Cemetery and the Custis-Lee antebellum mansion perched above it. I had no doubt he possessed one of the reserved parking spaces at the River Entrance, as well. But what caught my eye, as it surely was intended for every visitor, was the photo on the wall of Espy and the Secretary of Defense, both grinning like Cheshire cats. Yet, more telling, was the framed quote on the credenza.

Act with brutality, and close your hearts to pity.

A. Hitler.

I was reaching for my card and thinking that had to be the office credo, when he demanded, "What the hell's going on?" And while his tone was harsh, he kept his voice low. This discussion wasn't for other ears.

I placed my card on his desk, and began by telling him what I was sure he already knew. "We're conducting an investigation into the death of Midshipman Jeff Resnick.

"Damn it, I know that," he said looking down at my card. "Jerzy Shore? What the hell kind of name is that?"

"A little family joke."

He didn't respond, but his expression suggested it was a witless one, which momentarily set him squarely in my camp. "I don't have a lot of time," he said. "So let's get to the bottom line. Why are you asking questions about me?"

"As I said, it's part of the investigation."

"Investigation, my ass. The way I hear it, you've all but got me tagged for that plebe's death." And when I didn't refute it, he said, "Do you have any idea what you're doing?"

"Of course. I'm looking into the circumstances leading to Midshipman Resnick's death."

He rolled his eyes as if addressing an idiot. "I mean what you're doing to me."

"I'm not doing anything to you, Captain. I didn't just pick you out of the phone book. Your name came up as part of an official investigation."

We were still standing, our eyes locked, the large mahogany desk between us. Just as well, I thought. Without it we might soon be swinging at each other.

"Don't play games," he warned. "You're sullying my name, and I won't have that."

Sullying my name! Who talks like that? I wondered.

"You want to get to the bottom line, Captain? Fine," I said. "Did you have anything to do with Midshipman Resnick going into that tower?"

"What if I did?"

"Then I'd want to know if you were up there with him."

"Look, Shore, you're chasing your tail. Whatever happened is history. A tragic accident, to be sure. But an accident nevertheless. You read the report. If there was anything indicating otherwise it would've come out." Then, squaring his shoulders, he said, "I want this witch hunt stopped immediately."

"I'm sure you do, Captain. But, for the record, you haven't answered my questions."

He sighed. "Tell me why I should." And when I didn't respond, he said, "If you've got a shred of evidence linking me to this incident, tell me. Otherwise, cease and desist."

If I had been in uniform I'm sure he would have said, "That is all, Sailor. Dismissed." Instead he glanced at his watch.

"Mind if I sit?" I asked taking the chair without waiting for a reply.

"I don't have time for this nonsense. I called you here for one reason. I don't want my name kicked around town. Beyond that I have nothing more to say."

At least he didn't say sully again. I unbuttoned my jacket and crossed my legs. He needed to know I wasn't leaving any time soon. "Ever hear of the Green Bowlers?" I asked.

He laughed. "I don't believe this."

"You saying they don't exist?"

"Who's feeding you this nonsense? Of course they don't, you fool. It's a tale perpetuated by also-rans. Officers who think they should've been promoted beyond their abilities and want to believe they've been denied because of some secret society. What gets me is the damn story never dies. It's been around god knows how long, and I've yet to meet one officer with firsthand knowledge of it." Then, his patience fading, he asked, "So you think I'm a Green Bowler, is that it?"

"That's what I've heard. Which might explain why I didn't find your name in the investigation."

"Did it occur to you it's because I had nothing to do with that plebe's death?"

"Please answer the question. Are you a Green Bowler?"

He had yet to sit. "For the last time, Shore, there are no Green Bowlers. Now, having said that, I'm going to take a moment out of a very busy day to educate you on a more portentous issue, and then this meeting will be over."

"Please do."

"I'm referring to what this office is about. Do you know what our mission is, and the urgency of it?"

"I have an inkling."

Dropping into his chair, he said, "I don't think you do. Briefly, the barbarians are at the gate, Shore, and there are no more buffers. Time and distance are not what they were in the last century. Which means if we can't act in real time we're doomed."

He went on, "This office is the nation's last line of defense against an enemy that craves to put us back into the Stone Age. Another round of attacks like nine-eleven on the homeland will do just that." He was animated but in control, as if he'd delivered this little speech hundreds of times. "If you can break away from your ludicrous investigation long enough, I recommend reading the secretary's speech to the National

War College. In it you'll see there are far more important things to worry about than a decades-old accidental death." Tempering his voice, he concluded, "You really must cease this quixotic mission and pursue some real criminals."

"I'll concede this country's in extremis, and that we're facing a new and dangerous enemy, but that doesn't change a fundamental principle, Captain."

What principle?"

"It's not who's right, but what's right," I answered. "No one is above the law, Captain, no matter how noble his cause." He responded with a laugh and I lost it. "The Resnick boy may be dead, but I'm not. I am Jeff Resnick's advocate. I am the one who will do what he cannot. So please think about this. If you pushed that boy, or in any way contributed to his death, you can forget about the barbarians at the gate, because I am your worst enemy."

I had crossed the line, but I no longer cared. The pompous bastard had provoked me, and now it was my turn. Pointing to his photo with the Secretary of Defense, I said, "And I don't care who you know."

I was hoping he would say something, anything I could throw back at him. Instead, all I got was a slow burn.

"One final thought," I said standing. "You asked about evidence, Captain. Allow me to educate *you*. There is always evidence, even decades later. It sits there waiting for someone like me to come along, and what may have been overlooked or discounted then won't be this time, I promise you. Meanwhile, you'd be wise to take time from transforming our forces and acquaint yourself with Edmund Locard's Exchange Principle of Evidence. It's every bit as enlightening as the secretary's speech, which, by the way, I have read."

"You'd better leave now," he said smoothly.

I nodded. But before crossing the room, I glimpsed the photo again, and wondered which bull elephant was going to come down on poor Scully. Standing in the open doorway, I said, "I'll be back, Captain."

All heads turned my way. What they couldn't see was Espy and his grim expression.

"You're out of your league, Shore," he whispered.

I smiled as if I hadn't heard him. And as I passed the others, I said, "It's been a pleasure."

Eleven

After our little dustup I was pretty certain Espy was involved with Resnick's death, though not quite how. What convinced me was the flicker of concern in his eyes when I mentioned Locard's Principle as I was leaving. It was a dead giveaway.

Once again, there were phone messages when I arrived home. I knew one had to be Scully seeking feedback on my meeting with Espy. And with Carol's interest in the case, one would surely be hers. Expecting Scully's anxious voice, I pressed the playback button and went to the fish tank.

"You have three new messages," the robotic voice announced while I tossed a ration of food to the nine little guys shooting to the surface like piranhas, making me wonder if I had fed them yesterday. It wouldn't have been the first time I forgot, and decided I needed a system to remind me.

I never fancied fish, either as food or pets. For what little companionship they provided I'd have been better served hanging a painting or photograph on the wall to absorb the bad chi, as one guide book advised.

Nine fish were needed, there was no flexibility in the number, according to the guides, but strangely, whether I had live fish or an image of them didn't matter to some practitioners. Too bad I hadn't learned that before setting up the aquarium I thought, tossing in a second helping for good measure.

It would have been more convenient had they been heartier—I'd already replaced several. A dog, now that's a pet worth coming home to. But with my schedule the poor mutt would spend half his life in a boarding kennel. And while the fish lacked personality, they didn't care how often I left town or for how long, as long as the neighbor's kid fed them. They were eating hungrily, so I added a third serving.

The first message was someone offering to pressure wash everything I owned—house, fence, driveway, patio—all at a super discount because he just happened to be working my neighborhood. "Right," I said, eying the moss growing on the sides of the tank and wondering if he might consider pressure washing that. "I'll pass," I said, skipping to the next message.

"Hi, Jerzy. It's Carol. Or should I say Iceman?" She laughed and I smiled along with her. "If you get this before seven call me at the office. Thought we might have dinner. Any later, I'll be home. Bye."

I was no longer interested in hearing the third message.

"Yo, Iceman!" Scully shouted more anxiously than when last we spoke. "Call me when you get this."

"First Carol," I said, envisioning a candlelit dinner and wherever it might lead.

The master chief answered and connected me without a grilling.

"Hi. How's it going?" she said, her lilt suggesting we might be moving into a more comfortable routine.

"You mean, how was my meeting with Espy?" I replied.

"Okay," she said, "you caught me. Care to discuss it over a dish of linguini in Old Town?"

She could've proposed hot dogs on the Mall and I'd have leapt at the offer. But Old Town, with its brick walks and colonial gas lanterns, conjured up a more romantic image. "Sure."

"Good. Pick me up at eight. I'll make reservations." Then, before I could reply, she said, "Gotta go. Bye."

Still holding the phone, I looked over at the fish and gave them a thumbs-up. "Thanks, fellas."

Unlike Carol, Scully wanted my assessment now. "Do we have a case?" he asked.

"The guy's a weasel," I replied. "First, he tries intimidating me, then ridicules me and, finally, he threatens me."

"That's always a good sign."

"Yeah," I agreed. "He's worried."

"What'd he say?"

"It isn't so much what he said as how he reacted when I dropped the bit on him about trace evidence."

"He blinked," Scully offered with a slight laugh.

"Yeah. Suddenly he was trying to remember every-thing that happened a lifetime ago—looking into the past to figure out where he might've slipped up. Like they all do when you walk into their lives after so many years."

"I love it," Scully said with renewed enthusiasm.

I went on. "As the lawyers like to say, there's a degree of guilt there. If the bastard didn't actually push Resnick, he's connected somehow."

"What's your gut telling you?"

"I'm betting, at the least he got Resnick into Mahan, maybe even went into the tower with him."

"Good lad." I could tell he was getting into it now, enjoying the news and plotting what to do with it.

"Still, it's going to take leg work," I reminded him. "There's the autopsy report and, if I can run them down, the officer who conducted and wrote up the investigation and the JAG officer who reviewed it. And Resnick's roommates, if I'm going to do this properly."

Scully was no longer listening. "Sure, sure. Get on it," he said, the urgency now gone from his voice. "If you're lucky they won't be retired somewhere in Montana."

"Chief," I warned, "we're sure to get heat from SecDef on this, a lot of heat."

"No doubt." Then after a moment, he added, "Why don't you write up a preliminary report."

"A preliminary report?" I had never prepared one for a cold case before; never had reason to. I shook my head. This case had more twists than a pretzel.

Then thinking, what the hell, if he's willing to fight the brass, I can at least provide the ammo. "Sure," I said. "I'll get on it."

"Nothing formal. Just a rundown on what you've done and where you're taking it. Get it to me in the morning."

"It won't contain much more than what I've already told you," I cautioned.

"That's fine. Just some talking points if I get called in. I'll handle it from there."

"*If* you get called in! The jungle drums are beating, Chief. It's just a matter of time before you're hauled up before the big boys."

He laughed. "Okay. *When* I get called."

Something had changed, and I wish I knew what.

* * *

For dinner in Old Town I wore my navy blazer, khakis and a light blue shirt. I was aiming for a casual evening and hoping it might lead to something more than a hasty goodnight kiss at the door. Still, as I drove to Carol's I was a tangle of nervous energy; wondering if I was the only one fanning this spark, while doing my best to stifle the unsettled notion that perhaps I was being foolhardy and overly optimistic.

She greeted me with a warm smile and a tumbler of Scotch. "Here," she said pressing the glass into my hand. "Something for the weary warrior." Then just as quickly, she leaned in and kissed me, a soft promising kiss that did wonders for my spirits. In the next instant she was trotting upstairs and shouting over her shoulder, "Make yourself comfortable. I'll be down in a minute."

"Take your time," I said, enjoying the taste of her lipstick.

I heard her on the phone, and a moment later she was skipping downstairs. "We have a table at eight forty-five."

"Where?"

"Landini Brothers. Been there?"

I shook my head and she informed me the menu was northern Italian, which sounded wonderful, considering that lately I'd been squeezing in a quick bowl of chili at the Hard Times Café on the way to Sis's or, when pressed, grabbing a quarter pounder, fries and a shake at McDonald's. On the few nights I skipped the nursing home I usually treated myself to a less hurried meal at one of several diners in the area.

"You'll like it."

"Go there often?" I asked.

"It's one of my favorites."

"Do you have many? Favorites, that is?"

She shook her head. "Not in Old Town. But I know some fine trattorias in Italy. If we ever get there I'll show you around."

I liked the way this conversation was going. "You mean on another case?"

"Perhaps," she said with a wink that fired my imagination. Then, nodding at my glass, "Shall I top it off? We have time."

"Why not?" I was open to anything, even skipping dinner, if that was where we were headed.

"Rough day?" she asked as she poured.

"You want to hear about Espy now, or later?"

"Depends. Is there much to tell?" she asked, sliding in beside me.

"Not really."

"Then tell me now."

I took a long sip. "Well, he's what I expected," I said, and watched her cock her head.

"And just what were you expecting?"

When I said, "He's full of himself," she laughed.

"Modesty isn't part of Ron's DNA. I guess it's because no matter the difficulty, he always comes out on top. A modern-day Midas." Then, more to herself, "I often wondered how he'd take a fall."

I couldn't resist. "You just may find out this time around," I said, my bravado eliciting a raised eyebrow.

"You mean there's proof?" she asked, laying her hand on my arm.

And when I didn't reply, she tightened her grip. "What do you have? What've you learned?"

This is what I get for trying to impress her, I thought. As a diversion, I said, "I'm getting ahead of myself. What do you know about the Green Bowlers?"

She released me and said, "You're turning over a lot of rocks in this garden, Jerzy."

I couldn't be sure if she was being critical or warning me? "That's what I get paid to do. Is there such a group?" I persisted.

"I don't know. There could be."

"But you've heard of them."

She nodded.

"So, assuming they exist, how likely is it Espy's one of them?"

She thought a moment. "If he is, I doubt you'll find out. The scuttlebutt is it's a secret society, like the one at Yale both presidents Bush were said to belong to." She stood and smoothed her skirt. "It's getting late. Let's talk about it over dinner."

I gulped my drink and felt the flush that comes from booze on an empty stomach.

Outside, she took my arm, Espy and the Green Bowlers seemingly forgotten. The warmth of the day lingered, luring neighbors to their stoops, everyone taking in the sweet scents of spring.

"Relax," she said tugging my arm and slowing my pace. "It's only a few blocks."

I smiled. "I'd forgotten how fast I'd been running this past week."

Landini Brothers was a first-floor bistro set in what looked like one of the town's original colonial ware-houses. There were tables outside, but no takers this early in the season. I held the door, and as she entered, she said, "Reservations are in your name."

The place hadn't looked busy from the street, but inside, the bar and adjoining dining room held a lively crowd of well-dressed locals. Heads turned as we entered, a few lingering stares directed at Carol.

"Good evening," said the jacketed maitre d', a short dark fellow with an Hispanic accent. And to Carol, "Nice to see you again."

She returned the smile, while I said, "Two for Mister Shore."

"Your table's ready," he said without checking the reservation list, and we followed him into a quieter, less crowded room.

Everything on the menu looked appetizing, and since she was familiar with it I followed her suggestions. We settled into an unhurried dinner and, whether it was the soft lighting and the wine, or that she was being thoughtful, there was no further mention of Espy or the Green Bowlers, which suited me fine. Instead we talked about ourselves, with Carol telling me how it was growing up the only child of a naval aviator, who also happened to be an academy graduate and a retired vice admiral. As a third generation naval officer, she admitted to wanting to be the first female four-star, which explained a lot. At one point, she asked, "So, why aren't you married?"

I shrugged. "Never found the right person." She accepted that, but I suspect she knew I was lying.

There had been someone, of course, and not too many years back, either—someone about Carol's age—who I would have married in a New York minute if things hadn't gone inexplicably south. But I had long since discarded those memories. Well, as much as anyone can discard a roller coaster affair that took me from bliss to despair in a nanosecond.

Saying there had never been anyone was easier than talking about how we had met and fallen in love—not gradually, and not over time—but with the speed and intensity of a lightning strike. I say, *we fell in love*, but reflecting back I'm no longer sure how she felt. Though, at the time I thought I knew—right up to the day I drove her to the airport to visit her family in North Carolina. When I picked her up the following week she told me it was over between us. She offered no reason, just that it was finished. And though she cried when she said it—cried hard and long—she remained firm. There were a few subsequent dates at my urging, but they were awkward and pointless. She had made her decision, or complied with her family's wishes—I never knew which—and there was no turning back. I, of course, was devastated.

"Nobody, eh?" she persisted with a penetrating gaze.

"Nope. Nary a soul," I said. Then, to avoid further prodding, I asked, "And you? How about you?"

She smiled knowingly and sipped her wine. "Too busy making rank," she replied.

"Come on," I said, happy for the digression. "Show me an admiral, and I'll show you a spouse."

"Did you know that before the second war ensigns were discouraged from marrying after graduation?" And when I shook my head, she said, "The Navy reasoned you had enough on your plate without the distractions of a wife."

"That was then. Times have changed."

"The Navy hasn't," she countered. "Not much, anyway. The demands and sacrifices are still there, especially for a woman with my aspirations."

"That doesn't seem to stop the others. I mean those assembly line weddings in Annapolis after graduation."

She shook her head. "You can't tell midshipmen or ensigns anything. They know it all."

"Tell them what?"

"The poor odds of a successful marriage coupled with a career." And when I asked how poor, she informed me, "More than half fail." Noting my surprise, she said, "What do you think happens to a marriage when you transport a young bride who knows nothing about the Navy across three time zones, plant her in a strange town, and sail over the horizon for six or seven months. It's a miracle any survive."

The subject had me thinking of her and Espy. Despite her claims, I was sure they would've made it together. But then, I wouldn't be sitting there with her. "How about later on, after you rose in rank?"

Our waiter brought our espressos before she could reply, and the question went unanswered.

Notwithstanding our discussion on marriage, I was feeling pretty good about the evening as we walked from Landini's to the river. With fewer strollers around, we stood alone at the water's edge watching the Potomac ebb seaward. There was no moon, but the lights from the Woodrow Wilson Bridge down-river dancing on the surface provided a nice backdrop. It was a beautiful scene. When a breeze off the water made her shiver, I gave her my jacket.

Once back at her place, I watched her pour two snifters of Grand Marnier and wondered where the night was heading. I knew where I wanted it to go. The kiss earlier and the way she held my hand afterwards were promising signs, but I was still uncertain. A presumptive move might easily undo all that preceded it.

My doubts began to fade when she sat beside me. But then she reminded me, "You were going to tell me how it went with Ron."

"Seems a shame to spoil a nice evening," I replied. Her smile suggested we finish business before moving on to something else, and so I said, "When I asked if he'd been in the tower with Resnick, he ducked the question, telling me instead he was too busy saving the world to worry about some long-dead plebe, and that I needed to cease my witch hunt."

"Sounds like Ron," she said, his name rolling comfortably off her lips.

Why don't women say Jerzy like that? I wondered.

"When he was done telling me how important he is I got his attention by mentioning trace evidence."

She looked puzzled, and I explained about Locard's Principle; how everyone at a crime scene alters it, including the perpetrator, who inadvertently leaves evidence behind or takes it with him, concluding, "And it's that trace evidence that inevitably leads us to him."

She knitted her brow. "But decades later?"

"Well," I confessed, "I doubt we'll find trace evidence in the tower, though I'll look. But there's Resnick. Specifically, the clothes he wore that night and his other belongings. Now that we're looking at this as a possible homicide we're bound to see things that were overlooked earlier."

She was leaning forward, only inches away, her arm resting on the back of the sofa, her hand supporting her chin. "Like what? What could possibly be around after all these years?"

"Well, his journal, for one thing."

"His journal?"

"I've skimmed it, and the boy had serious concerns about certain upperclassmen," I said.

"All plebes have those concerns."

I let that pass, and said, "We'll also look for fibers and hairs."

"And where do you expect to find them?"

"On his uniform."

"I don't understand. NCIS has his uniform?" I could see she wasn't buying it, or didn't want to.

"We have access to it." Then, noting her puzzlement, I said, "His parents have everything packed away, including the clothes he wore the night he went over the railing." I didn't know if they had, but I threw it in anyway. "You'd be amazed at what we're capable of analyzing nowadays."

She was already ahead of me. "Did you see the actual clothes?"

Again, another white lie. "They've got his entire sea bag. He was their only child," I said. Then, to cover myself, I told her, "But even without his uniform there are other means of building a case against the good captain."

She'd been cradling her glass in her lap and now she set it aside and edged closer. "*Building* a case?"

"That's what I do, Carol. I collect evidence— direct, indirect, circumstantial—and I use it to build a case," I said, adding, "It isn't black magic."

"It seems so tenuous."

Enjoying her full attention, I said, "I'll find out where Espy was when Resnick went over the rail, or more precisely, where he wasn't. If he wasn't in his room at that hour, he'll have some explaining to do."

"How after all this time can you determine if he left his room that night?"

"This is a homicide investigation," I reminded her, "and whoever provides false testimony places himself in serious jeopardy. Loyalty only goes so far."

Detecting a hint of sadness, I worried that she regretted having set this case in motion. If so, she didn't linger on it. A moment later our lips touched.

TWELVE

We kissed tentatively, and in the next instant she was straddling me, her arms locked around my neck, her body pressing against mine. When I could take it no longer, I suggested we relocate upstairs.

"Not yet," she gasped.

Sadly, the mood was broken, and she soon slipped away.

"It's late," she said, "and I have to get up early." Not wanting it to end, I reached for her and she shook her head. "I need time. This isn't something I do—meet a man and rush to bed with him."

We were at opposite ends of the sofa, and from the looks of it that's how it was going to stay.

"Well, neither do I," I said, trying to coax her back. "That is, I don't fall into *women's* arms easily, either," I said, drawing a laugh. "What I really mean is please don't think it's just a sex thing with me." And when she frowned, I quickly added, "Though that's certainly a factor. But the truth is I'm attracted to you. I think I have been from day one."

"Then let's not spoil this." She stood and pushed her skirt down.

"Couldn't we discuss it?" I said with a boyish grin.

Her gaze fell to the source of my distress, and she said, "You need to go home and take a cold shower."

"How 'bout we take one together?"

She seemed to consider it, but held firm. "Like I said, tomorrow's a work day."

Not one to give up easily, I said, "Don't worry about me. I set my own hours."

"Nice try." She had my hand and was pulling me up. "But you really must leave."

As a final ploy I tried the hangdog routine, but she wasn't buying that either. And so, following her to the door, I asked, "You working Saturday?"

"I'll let you know," she said before pressing in for a final kiss. When we parted, she glanced down and said, "Bring your friend."

"I never leave home without him."

She was still grinning when she placed her hand on my chest and pushed me gently into the night. "Drive carefully," she whispered before closing the door.

I replied with a weak nod, but rather than head for my car, I stood there for a disquieting moment trying to sort things out.

* * *

My hormones were still screaming when I pulled into the driveway, and I knew without that cold shower and a healthy dose of Scotch I'd be tossing all night. But first there was the answering machine. It could only be Carol, calling to say she'd reconsidered and would I please hurry back. I pressed the playback button expecting her apology, and heard the stressed out voice of the night supervisor at the nursing home.

"Mister Shore, there's been an incident. Please call us as soon as you receive this."

My first thought was Sis had suffered another stroke, this one fatal, which is what the doctors predicted might occur based on her previous lifestyle and our family's medical history. Having studied up on strokes when she entered into my care, I learned that subsequent strokes were common among stroke victims, and many of those were fatal. And so I was prepared for this eventuality, or so I thought. Yet despite our sibling differences, the prospect of losing my only remaining relative left me feeling oddly numb.

Forgetting there was no one at the switchboard at this late hour, my frustration turned to anger while waiting for someone to answer. I thought, *there's been an incident*, could mean anything. You could never tell with the staff. They were masters at covering themselves whenever a problem arose. What troubled me was that they had never called at this hour before, or with such urgency.

"This is Mister Shore," I blurted when the nurse finally picked up. "You called about my sister Dinah?"

"Oh, Mister Shore. We've been trying to reach you for the past hour."

"Well you got me," I said cutting her off. "What's the problem? Has something happened to my sister?"

What followed was a disjointed exchange as she quickly assured me, "Miss Shore is fine. But not Bernice…"

"Bernice?" Why the hell are you calling me about Bernice?"

"She ate your sister's candy, and— well— we don't know—."

"Candy? What candy?" The night shift came on after visiting hours, so I had never met her, and, worse, had no idea what she was talking about.

"It happened so suddenly," she said, and I heard her voice quiver.

"Calm down," I said, willing myself to do the same.

She took a breath, and said, "We called 9-1-1."

"Called 9-1-1? For who?"

"When Bernice became deathly ill."

"Not my sister?"

"No. Like I said, you're sister's fine. Just Bernice."

"So why call me?" I asked again. "What's this got to do with my sister?"

"Your sister," she said, "alerted us by pressing the call button in her room after Bernice ate the candy."

"I didn't bring my sister candy. You mean the ice cream?"

"No. The candy," she insisted, her voice steadier now. "The box of candy on your sister's nightstand. According to your sister, Bernice ate a piece and fell ill."

"Where is she now?"

"The hospital."

"My sister?"

"No. Bernice. Your sister's upstairs. We moved her to a different room. It's just temporary. Till the police finish and we clean up the mess."

"Police?"

"Yes. They told us to move her and not let anyone in the room."

"Look," I said, "I'm coming right over."

"Good idea. I'm sure they'll want to talk to you."

* * *

As I raced across town I thought of Espy's threats, and resolved to pistol whip the bastard if he had anything to do with this.

An unoccupied Arlington County patrol car was at the main entrance when I arrived, its red and blue lights still flashing. I parked and bolted for the door. I had my badge out as I entered and flashed it at the uniform in the lobby. "I'm here about my sister, Miss Shore," I said before he could ask who I was.

"You're gonna want to talk to the detective," he replied, nodding at a nearby office and the heavyset guy hunched over the desk working the phone.

"Right after I check on my sister," I said over my shoulder as I headed for the nurses' station and the short fragile woman behind it.

I'd learned over the years most night supervisors took this shift to avoid dealing with demanding administrators and nettlesome family members. Understandably, they tended to be introverts who didn't do well under pressure.

"I'm Mister Shore," I said as I approached.

To her credit this one seemed to have pulled herself together. More composed now than when we spoke, she said, "Miss Shore's upstairs, in room 215. You're welcome to go up, but she's asleep. I just checked on her myself."

"What the hell's going on?" I snapped, causing her to flinch.

"It's like I told you. Bernice became ill after eating your sister's candy. If your sister hadn't alerted us, poor Bernice might've died. That's really all I know, Mister Shore. The police are here because the emergency crew called them. There's a detective Barone using the front office. It's probably best you talk with him."

"I will. But first tell me about this candy. Where'd she get it?"

She shrugged. "We assumed from you. It was on her nightstand. A miniature box of chocolates. The police have it now."

"What kind of candy?"

She shrugged. "I don't know. One of those samplers with about six pieces of chocolate."

"Okay," I said. "I'll talk to them after checking on my sister."

I took the stairs two at a time rather than the snail-elevator, as the residents called it, and found

Sis sleeping soundly, as the nurse had said. They had moved her in with two other residents, both asleep. Looking around, I decided there was no point waking her and disturbing the others. And so, with a thousand questions and my stomach in knots, I eased out and headed for Detective Barone.

He was still on the phone, and with a nod directed me to a chair.

"Frank Barone," he said in the way of an introduction when he'd finished.

"Agent Jerzy Shore," I replied, offering my ID. "What's going on?"

He was close to fifty—putting him about my age—and slow talking, with flat eyes that stayed glued to mine. "I know you're upset, but let me ask the questions. Okay?"

I could see he wasn't being a wise-ass, just trying to do his job. I nodded. "Go ahead."

"The lady who ate the candy was looking after your sister?"

"Bernice, yeah. My sister's one of her patients."

He grunted as if he already knew that. "What can you tell me about the candy we found in your sister's room?"

"Absolutely nothing. I don't know anything about it."

"You didn't bring it?"

"I just said that." I saw him bristle but I didn't care. I knew the procedure, but I wasn't in the mood for it. When he didn't respond, I said, "No, I didn't bring it. Sis doesn't eat sweets. I mean, she likes them but because of the weight problem—you know, being confined to a wheelchair without being able to exercise—we restrict her intake. Excess weight will stress her heart and could bring on another stroke. So we watch her diet."

"We?"

"Me and the staff. She gets Jello and fruit for dessert. No cake or ice cream," I explained. "Occasionally, I bring a treat, but never a box of chocolates."

"How do you know it was a box of chocolates?"

"The supervisor."

"So, if it wasn't from you where'd it come from? Another family member?"

I shook my head. "I'm it. There's no one else."

He looked at me for a long moment, but I wasn't playing the game. And when I didn't offer up any more info, he asked, "So you got no idea where it came from?"

I thought of Espy again but decided not to mention him. Not without being sure. "No, not a clue." Then I remembered Joe. "Wait a sec."

He raised an eyebrow.

"Some guy's been talking to Sis. I don't know him. Never met or saw him. All's I know is she said he's been around a few times."

"What's his name?"

"She calls him Joe."

He jotted it down. "Joe who?"

I shook my head. "That's all, just Joe. She said he stops by to talk, but I couldn't get any more out of her. That's how it is with stroke victims. At least it is with Sis. She'll tell me something and then I have to pull the rest out of her." I didn't see any point in telling him about our strained relationship. It was personal and none of his business.

"And you couldn't get any more about this Joe fella?"

"No. Whenever I tried she moved on to something else. I figured he was a visitor, one of the family members. That's how a lot of them do it—stop by and say a few words to the folks they see sitting in the lobby or other public areas. It breaks the monotony and lets 'em know somebody's interested. I do it myself. It doesn't take much effort, and it puts a smile on their faces."

His gaze wandered out to the lobby. "Must be tough," he said.

"It isn't easy," I said, thinking of Sis parked in that wheelchair, and no prospects of ever getting out of it.

Returning to Joe, he asked, "You check around? See if anybody knows this fella?"

I nodded. "Yeah, but no luck. Not even Bernice, and not much gets past her. To be honest, I didn't try too hard. Like I said, I figured he's a relative of one of the residents, and I'd run into him one of these days."

The interview went on like that until Barone seemed satisfied I didn't know anything and wasn't holding anything back. At which point, I asked about Bernice. "How's she doing?"

"Still in emergency," he said with the same fixed expression that made reading him difficult. "We got one of our people with her. That's who was on the phone. They've stabilized her, but she's not awake yet."

"And the candy?"

"We're checking it."

It was clear he wasn't going to disclose any more, so I didn't ask. The last thing he would do is share info with a suspect—which is what I was at the moment—like, if they had lifted prints from the box or its contents, or what the lab had learned. Hell, he wouldn't even tell me the brand of candy if I asked. I know I wouldn't if it was my case, which left me pretty much out of the loop. But that didn't have to be permanent. In the morning I'd find out who at the office had an in with the Arlington PD. Meanwhile, I would have to discover on my own if Espy was connected to this in any way. And, God help him if he was.

THIRTEEN

I walked in, tossed my jacket aside and headed for the Scotch I hadn't gotten to earlier. Now more in need of that drink, I poured, swallowed, and poured again. Without the insistent beep of the answering machine the only sound came from the steady hum of the aquarium, reminding me the fish needed feeding, but they could wait. I had some serious thinking to do.

Number one on my agenda was figuring out why someone had targeted Sis, a harmless soul, which told me it was either the random act of some fruitcake or, more troubling, someone sending me a message. If it was random, then the Arlington PD was the one to handle it. It had the manpower and resources for the job. But if I was the target, then I was better positioned to work the problem, which meant coming up with a list of suspects. The trouble was, only one name came to mind—Captain Ron Espy. Yet, as much as I was growing to dislike him, I couldn't see him doing this, not because he wasn't capable, rather that he was too precise to leave tainted candy around for an innocent like Bernice to pick up. That was more the work of an amateur.

I knocked back another Scotch, closed my eyes and let the warmth work its magic. It felt good, good enough to pour another. This one I sipped. It was too expensive to guzzle. I kicked off my shoes, put my feet on the ottoman, and began parsing the problem, trying to imagine who other than Espy was reaching out to me, and why.

I must have fallen asleep holding that thought, because the next thing I knew I was jarred by the phone.

It was Scully, shouting the instant I picked up. "I just heard from Arlington PD. You okay?"

"What time is it?" I mumbled through a dry mouth.

"Six thirty. What's going on?" he asked with concern.

"I wish I knew, Chief. I've been trying to figure it out, and the only connection I come up with is Espy. But it doesn't make sense."

"Why Espy?"

"To divert me, get me off his back. But I can't get beyond that. I was just in his office less than twenty-four hours ago laying Resnick's death at his feet, and now he's targeting me? It doesn't track."

"He could be running scared."

"No. He's angry, not scared." This is weird, I thought. I'm ready to exclude the one logical lead.

"Who then? Who else is out there?"

"No one I can think of. Yet I can't see him doing this."

"Too amateurish?"

"Yeah."

"Well, it'd be foolish not to run it down," he said. And when I didn't reply, he said, "Confront him. Get in his face and lay it out."

That didn't seem like a good idea, that is, accuse the guy I'm building a case against of going after my sister without any evidence. There had to be a better way, but at this early hour, I wasn't seeing it. I was tired and my head throbbed.

Sensing my reluctance, Scully said, "I suppose we can take another approach."

"Yeah?"

"Tip off the Arlington PD."

"To what?" I asked.

"That he's the subject of a homicide investigation, which he may be trying to de-rail. Fill them in on the details and let them put some uniforms on him. It might make him do something stupid. It's worked before."

That surprised me, and I countered, "You know what this'll do to the elephants?"

"What are the alternatives? You said he deserves to be looked at."

Somewhere along the way we'd switched roles, and now I was the cautious one. "You think the SecDef's going to sit still for that? Letting us hang one of his key staff members out to dry for a botched attempted homicide that might easily be the work of some fruitcake?"

"And on that supposition you'll blindside the police in their investigation?" Scully countered.

"I don't want to blindside anyone. I'm just not comfortable bringing them in when I haven't come up with anything conclusive yet."

"You said it yourself. Lacking other leads, Espy's at the top of the list. Don't you think they need to know that?"

"I guess you're right," I said without much conviction.

"Of course I am. By the way, that gal— the one who ate the candy— what's her name?"

"Bernice."

"Yeah. Well, according to Arlington PD, they stabilized her. From the looks of it she ingested a fairly large dose. But she's young enough and strong enough, they figure she'll be okay."

"What was it?" I asked, relieved at the news.

"Looks to be the antidepressant Amitriptyline," he said. "The stuff they give recovering alcoholics to relieve withdrawal depression. I'm told it isn't lethal unless administered to someone in a weakened state and on meds, like your sister. Whoever used it was pretty clever."

"Yeah? How so?"

"SOB laced just the one chocolate."

"The one she picked."

"Yeah. The other three were clean. That way there'd be nothing tying it to the others once she ate it. Without a witness it would've looked like she suffered a heart attack, and the candy would've been overlooked. Smart, uh?"

"Now that's something Espy might do," I said, my anger rising again. "How'd they ID the poison with the evidence consumed?"

"He wasn't that clever. There are traces on the wrapper."

I took out Detective Barone's card and set it on the table.

"So, what do you want to do?" Scully asked.

"Guess I'll call Arlington PD. That's what you want, isn't it?"

"Jerzy, it isn't what *I* want, it's what needs to be done," he said. Then, before hanging up, "Let me know if I can help."

He was the second one offering me help, Carol being the first. I should have felt reassured, but I didn't.

Before phoning the nursing home, I showered, dressed, and gulped two cups of coffee. I needed time to deal with the nagging feeling I was being manipulated.

When the day supervisor answered she sounded more stressed than usual. No doubt Barone and his troops had the place in turmoil. Considering the daily demands of caring for nearly two hundred invalids, it wouldn't take much.

"Your sister's fine," she assured me. "She slept through the night and is having breakfast in the dining room." Then, her voice cracking, she said, "First thing she did when she awoke was to ask for Bernice. We had to tell her we don't know her status. Poor thing's quite upset, as we all are." After a moment, she said, "It's frightening to think what might've happened had Miss Shore not been there for Bernice."

I agreed, but I was equally grateful Sis hadn't eaten the chocolate. "I assume the police are still there."

"Oh, yes," she said with more than a trace of exasperation. "They're doing their best to stay out of our way."

"What about Detective Barone?"

"He seems to be everywhere," she said with a heavy sigh. "I think he's with the administrator now."

"When you see him," I said, "please tell him I'm on my way over. That I need to speak with him."

"I will. Wait! Here he comes. You can tell him yourself."

I heard her call to him, and a moment later, he had the phone. "Barone," he said. His voice was gravelly, his manner abrupt.

"Morning. This is Jerzy Shore. We need to talk."

"Okay," is all he said.

I still had two calls to make, and when I told him I could be there in thirty minutes he said that would be fine.

I hung up and punched in Carol's number. The master chief said she was out of the office, and that he expected her back by nine thirty. It was nearly eight. I told him I would call back after ten. A moment later I was talking to the icy blonde in Espy's office. "Is he in?" I asked, after identifying myself.

She was no friendlier this time. "He'll be in meetings all day. Would you care to leave a message?"

Having overheard her phone etiquette during my first visit, I knew she could be more congenial. Obviously, I didn't rate, which was okay, since I wasn't out to win friends. "When's he break for lunch?" I asked.

"The captain doesn't break for lunch," she informed me.

"I'll take my chances. I'll be there at noon," I said.

"Agent Shore!" she said before I could hang up. "He won't return until two."

"Then two it is," I said, and hung up.

On the way out I remembered the fish. A quick glance confirmed they were alive and doing what fish do. I tossed in a generous amount of food, probably more than necessary, and left.

* * *

To the staff's credit, it was pretty much business as usual at the nursing home despite the intrusion of police and crime lab team. I found Sis with several other residents grouped around the upright piano in the second floor lounge. They were singing "Michael Row the Boat Ashore". Seeing me, the music therapist, a portly woman who headed the choir at a nearby Baptist church, smiled and waved me over. Including family members in group activities was routine, which was fine, but not today.

I declined with a smile while extracting Sis, and was relieved to see her looking well, though noticeably stressed—a small price to pay, considering what might have happened.

"I thought you'd like to know Bernice is going to be all right," I said, and watched her brighten. "She'll probably remain in the hospital a few days but she'll be fine. She was very lucky you were there to call the nurse."

Now she smiled.

"Who gave you the candy?"

She shrugged. "I don't know."

Strange, I thought. "You have no idea where it came from? How about that Joe fellow? The one who's been stopping by, could he have left it?"

Her eyes widened and she tensed again. "I said I don't know." Sis could be obstinate at times.

"All right, don't worry about it," I said, patting her shoulder. "If you think of anything, please let me know. Okay?"

She had already moved on. "When am I getting my room back?"

"Don't you like your new room?" I said, thinking I might persuade her to remain on the second floor, where I thought it safer. "You've got a nicer view."

She was having none of it, and with a hard stare, she said, "I don't want to live in a goddamn dormitory. I'm paying for a single room on the first floor. And, damn it, that's what I want."

"I'll talk to the supervisor. I'm sure it won't be long, probably today, tomorrow the latest."

"It better not be any longer."

Amazing, how articulate Sis can be when she wants, I thought as I left her.

* * *

It was past nine when I found Barone in the basement. He was towering above a contingent of kitchen workers who looked more fearful of being deported than being part of his investigation. Knowing he'd seen me, I waited at a discrete distance until he finished with them, and when he had they scattered like roaches under a light.

"You're late," he said clenching a well-chewed unlit cigar stub between his teeth.

His cool demeanor surprised me. It wasn't what I expected from a brother uniform. But then, judging from his puffy eyes and beard stubble, I chalked it up to lack of sleep. Instead of leading me to a less trafficked area, we stood near the two elevators, where every few minutes we were forced to sidestep staff and residents.

"So," I said, "I hear Bernice is stabilized and we're looking at Amitriptyline as the weapon."

"Yeah. She was lucky, but not as lucky as your sister," he said, to which I agreed. "So what's your read on this?" he asked, his dark eyes holding mine, a tactic that could be unnerving to the uninitiated.

Instead of coming right out about Espy, I said, "I spoke with Sis this morning about this Joe fella, but she couldn't tell me anything—or wouldn't. I can't be sure. I sensed she didn't appreciate my suggesting he might have something to do with this. How about you? Any luck running him down?"

Barone shook his head. "Zip. No description and no leads. You're the only one who seems to have anything on him, you and your sister."

I didn't appreciate him trying to rattle me, but rather than react, I said, "There may be someone else worth looking at."

He shifted his cigar, rolling it across his bottom lip. "Another mystery guest?"

"Look," I said without hiding my resentment, "that was my sister that almost got it. I'm trying to help you."

"Go on," he said with a coolness that had me rethinking why I had opened this door.

Reluctantly, I briefed him on the Resnick case, and my concerns about Espy trying to turn my head.

"Who is this guy?" he asked. And when I told him, he said, "You like playing with the big boys?"

"Not especially," I said, thinking I'll never warm to this guy. "But I go where the leads take me. And in the Resnick case they seem to be pointing in his direction."

"And so you figure he's telling you to get out of his way?"

I wasn't as convinced of that as Scully was, yet I nodded. "It's a stretch, but other than this guy Joe, he's the only lead I've got."

Barone took it in without comment, and I knew he was thinking maybe I was the one blowing smoke. Still, I had put Espy in his sights, which is what Scully wanted. With nothing more to impart, I wished him luck and headed back upstairs.

Before leaving, I stopped by Sis's first floor room for a look-see, but the door was padlocked and barred with yellow crime scene tape. As I crossed the patio to my car I turned and walked over to Sis's window midway down the wing. The aluminum screen was unhooked at the bottom. A closer inspection didn't reveal any pry marks, and I wondered how long it had been that way. At waist level, it was easy for someone to pull the screen away, duck under it, and raise the window enough to lean in and set the candy on Sis's nightstand. It wouldn't take a minute and, done at night, would be barely noticeable.

"Yeah, we thought of that," Barone said from behind. "No need for him to enter the building."

I swung around, letting the screen fall back in place. "For a big guy you got a soft walk."

He grinned. "When I have to." Then nodding at the row of windows, he said, "If you check you'll see all the screens are hanging loose from their top hinges. The cleaning crew likes 'em that way. Saves time when washing the windows," he explained.

"So much for security," I said. Then, noting the streaked panes, "When is that, once a year?"

"Three times according to the housekeeper. Spring, summer and fall. Good thing we already dusted for prints, or we'd have yours."

"Sorry. I have to remember it's your crime scene."

For the first time his expression softened and, in what could pass for genuine empathy, he said, "She was my sister, I'd be doing the same thing."

I nodded. Maybe I was reading him wrong. "So when's she getting her room back?"

"Probably after supper. Got a few more things need checking first. Meanwhile, I suggest you talk to management about them screens. From what I hear, you folks are paying enough to have 'em secured."

"Count on it," I said. "So you're about finished here?"

He shrugged. "We finish when we finish."

My kind of guy, I mused. Yet, as I headed for my car I wondered again if putting him onto Espy was wise.

As if reading my mind, he called after me, "You going to be talking to this Espy guy?"

I stopped and turned. "This afternoon. Two o'clock."

"What're you going to tell him?"

"That if he had anything to do with this he made a big mistake."

Barone just nodded.

As I drove away I saw him call to one of the groundskeepers and point toward the window. The guy was thorough, I'd give him that.

* * *

Once back at the office, I tried Carol again.

"Hey," she said with a happy-to-hear-from-you lilt that had me thinking she regretted shoving me out the door last night. "How you holding up?"

"Not too good," I said before giving her a rundown of all that had happened with Sis.

"That's horrible. What kind of sick person would do such a thing? Thank God she's unharmed. And the other poor lady, you said she'll be fine?"

"They stabilized her, but I don't know about the aftereffects. Chances are they'll be minimal." I had checked out the drug and learned it was unlikely young, healthy people would suffer any serious or long term consequences, provided they weren't consuming drugs that interacted with the Amitriptyline. At worst, it appeared Bernice would experience temporary lightheadedness and confusion. "Look," I said, "we need to talk. How about lunch?"

"Can't. I'll be back in the office by one."

"Okay. See you then."

Fourteen

I arrived early and was standing outside Carol's office hoping to catch her before she got involved in other matters, when she and a four-star emerged from a doorway at the far end of the hall where they paused momentarily before walking slowly toward me, he jabbing the air with his fist, and she leaning into him like an anxious shadow. Others passing by knew enough to hasten their step and give them a wide berth.

Their conversation concluded abruptly about fifty feet from me, with the admiral patting her shoulder before disappearing into another office. Carol continued on with a furrowed expression, her eyes cast down. When she finally looked up and saw me, she broke into a quick smile. "Hi. Been waiting long?"

"Just got here." And as she reached for the door, I said, "Mind if we take a stroll?"

She frowned. "Sounds serious."

"I've had better days," I said, steering her toward the inner A-ring and the courtyard beyond.

She seemed to understand, and we walked on in silence until we were outside, away from curious ears.

The high walls blocked what little breeze came off the Potomac, and I immediately felt uncomfortably warm. Rather than taking one of the benches close to the food court, we followed the perimeter road, where we would have more privacy.

She asked about Sis, and I said she was okay, explaining that she was more concerned about Bernice than herself. "Look," I said with some misgivings, "I'm not sure you want to hear this but there's a possibility our boy Espy was involved."

She stopped and said, "With the attempt on your sister's life? Involved how?"

"I'm thinking he may be responsible for placing the candy in her room."

"You can't be serious."

Her response threw me, and I countered with probably too much edge in my voice. "I'm dead serious."

"Ron would never do that."

"Are we talking about the same guy you fingered for Resnick's death?"

She lowered her voice as several people drew near. "I'm *not* defending him. But I can't see how this incident with your sister has anything to do with Jeff. Why on earth would Ron want to harm her?"

Hearing her take his side angered me further, and I snapped back, "I'll tell you why. How about he's trying to intimidate me? From what I hear he's pretty good at that. Or, he wants me off his back? He's certainly made that very clear. Or that he's a sick SOB? Or, having done it once he's capable of doing it again?"

I was prepared to go on, but I was drawing unwanted glances from passersby.

"Let's walk," she suggested, and we fell in far enough behind two Marines to ensure they didn't hear us.

"I suppose from your perspective it seems feasible," she conceded. "But I know Ron, and he'd never do something like this. You must believe me." And when I didn't reply, she looked at me and asked, "What are you going to do?"

We had completed a half turn around the courtyard and were heading for the corridor we had exited from. "I'm going to confront him," I said as we stepped into the shadow of the building.

"When?"

"Two o'clock today, his office."

"Jerzy, is that wise? What do you hope to accomplish?"

"I want to see his reaction."

"Is that what you did last time?"

I nodded. "He was hiding something then. He's easy to read."

"Don't do it," she said. "Don't pull him into this. He had nothing to do with your sister or her aide."

"You seem pretty convinced."

"I am."

"It's too late," I said.

Stopping again, she gripped my arm, and said, "What do you mean?"

I hadn't planned on mentioning Barone and the Arlington PD, and when I did she exploded.

"Jesus Christ!"

Her outburst drew the attention of three soldiers coming our way and she fell quiet. When they were gone, she looked around and said through a clenched jaw, "What were you thinking? I can't believe you did that. Jerzy, you've crossed the line."

Now I was on the defensive. "What are you talking about? I don't have any jurisdiction over the nursing home. This is an Arlington PD matter. And for all they know, I could be the perp."

She wasn't buying it. "But bringing Ron into it, and telling them about the Resnick case... They have no business in this." She was rubbing her forehead. "This is a Navy investigation. At least it was."

"Look," I said, feeling no need to defend myself, "Espy doesn't have any more rights than a seaman." But she wasn't listening, her thoughts obviously elsewhere.

After a brief moment, she said more to herself than to me, "I have to go," and, turning, hurried off.

"I would have been derelict if I hadn't alerted them," I said catching up to her. "In a case like this the police have to look at everyone." She remained stone silent, and I couldn't tell if she heard me. "NCIS is ready to take the hits," I added.

It wasn't until we were inside that she noticed I was still with her. "I need to get back," she said. And when I offered to accompany her, she said, "Don't you have to meet Ron?"

"I have time," I said.

She shrugged and continued on, no doubt anxious to alert her boss and that four-star I'd seen her with earlier, which, no doubt, would set off a series of phone calls, one of which was sure to conclude with Scully, thereby completing the circle.

We continued on at a quick pace, neither of us speaking. When we reached her office, I asked, "Will I see you tonight?"

The question seemed to surprise her. And as she studied me, I felt a twinge of regret for turning Barone onto Espy. Then, to my surprise, her face softened and she said, "How's nine?"

"Nine's good," I replied with a tentative smile.

"See you then," she said, and stepped inside.

With time to spare, I detoured to a nearby snack bar for a coffee and a few quiet moments to think about what had just happened between us, and why I was drawn to this woman. But there were no clear answers. And so, sitting there with her photo, I decided that whatever the reason, I wasn't going to walk away, and I hoped she wouldn't either. Ten minutes later I was heading for the lion's den certain of at least one thing—the jungle drums were beating.

This time I wasn't asked to show my ID. The taut lines around the receptionist's mouth and her stiff movements as she led me to Espy's office suggested trouble, big trouble. She knocked, and I heard Espy's dry voice. "Enter." But rather than opening the door and showing me in, she stepped aside as if wanting no part of what was about to happen. I noticed, too, the two majors were hunching over their computers and doing their best not to look my way. From all appearances it was not a happy time in Mudville.

Espy came around from his desk as I closed the door behind me. Seeing him riled me and, holding his gaze, I stormed across the room, meeting him midway. In the next instant, I was shoving him. "You sonofabitch," I shouted.

He threw an off-balanced punch that brushed my jaw, and before he swung again I kicked his foot from beneath him and was on him as he dropped.

He fell hard, and with my knee pressing into his chest, he hissed, "You're in big trouble. Don't make it worse."

"*I'm* in trouble?" I said, feeling the handle of my revolver cutting into my side.

"I had nothing to do with your sister. Now get the hell off me," he ordered.

We were like two schoolyard kids staring each other down, neither wanting to yield. He knew I couldn't keep him there for long, and so he didn't resist.

"I don't believe you," I said, before hauling him up and pressing him into the chair I'd used during my first visit.

"Believe what the hell you want," he said, his fists still balled. "But you have no fucking business setting me up as a suspect with the cops."

"News travels fast around here," I said, thinking Barone hadn't had time to contact him, so it had to be Carol.

He took a deep breath and said, "What the hell's going on? First, you accuse me of the plebe's death, and now of attacking your sister."

"You don't see a pattern?"

"The only pattern is that for some idiotic reason you have me in your crosshairs."

"It isn't by accident," I said more calmly now.

"You're doing irreparable damage here, Shore. This lunacy has to stop."

"So you deny hiring or directing someone to poison her?"

He heaved a sigh. "Why in god's name would I do that?"

"The why's the reason you're a suspect, Captain. So if you have something to say this is a good time to say it."

Another sigh, this one deeper. "This whole thing is ludicrous. What possible motive would I have?"

"You're worried I'll tie you to Resnick's death, and you'll do whatever's necessary to derail my investigation, which is exactly what Arlington PD will conclude."

"So why aren't they here instead of you?" he said just before we heard a tentative knock.

We both turned, and I could tell from the alarm in his eyes he expected the police to walk in. Instead, his secretary peered in. "Your meeting with the Secretary of Defense has been moved up, sir. They'd like you there now," she said before quickly backing out.

"Are we finished?" he said, pushing past me to retrieve several folders from atop his desk, and stuffing them into a leather briefcase.

"Not by a long shot," I replied.

He paused, looked hard at me, and locking his elbows, leaned on his desk, and said, "A final word of caution, Shore. If you continue this game, I'll have your balls and your badge on that wall. Meanwhile, I suggest telling your friends in Arlington to look elsewhere."

"I can't do that," I countered. "You're my main suspect."

"This meeting's over," he said grabbing his briefcase. "Get out."

* * *

When I reached my office everyone I met immediately informed me that Scully wanted to see me ASAP.

It's great to be popular, I mused as I headed upstairs.

"He's expecting me," I said without waiting for my least favorite co-worker to clear me.

My sudden interruption had both Scully and a Navy captain I hadn't met before turning in my direction. "Excuse me, Chief," I said backing out, while Miss Receptionist-of-the-Year grinned. "I'll come back at a better time."

"No, no," he said waving me back in. "This concerns you."

Where are all these captains coming from? I thought. I had encountered more brass in a week than in all my years with the Navy. And, like the others, this one appeared deadly serious; no doubt due to the Resnick case, which I concluded could wear down a shipload of captains. Of course, the negative chi swirling around Scully's office didn't help any.

"Agent Shore," Scully said once I closed the door, "this here's Captain Pickett Lumpkin, Deputy Chief of Information." His tone was noncommittal, revealing none of the urgency that had me rushing there, a tactic he often used when dealing with outsiders. "We've been discussing your case."

So now it's my case again. A surprise, considering all the rudder orders I'd been receiving.

I nodded and slid into a chair while Lumpkin extended his hand.

"How do you do, Agent Shore?" he said with a pleasant southern drawl.

I returned his firm handshake. "I have a feeling you're about to tell me," I replied, knowing an unexpected visit from a public relations four-striper could mean only one thing; the press was about to pounce on us—more correctly, on me.

He offered a wry grin and immediately confirmed my suspicions. "As I was telling your chief, we have a problem."

A quick side-glance at Scully gave no hint of what that problem might be, and so I waited for Lumpkin to tell me.

"We received a query from the *Washington Post* about your investigation into the Resnick affair," he said without elaboration.

My first thought was of the Resnicks and their initial threat to go public, and my assurance to Scully after meeting with them that they wouldn't. Amazing how quickly things spin out of control.

"And since we didn't know anything about it," he continued, "I naturally called over here to set up a powwow."

A powwow? I felt the negative chi slamming into my neck and immediately rolled my shoulders. "I don't get it," I said. "Why's the *Post* interested in a decades-old accidental death?"

Lumpkin's expression didn't change as he explained, "Agent Shore, it's not Resnick, but the person you're investigating that's causing the stir."

I looked at Scully again and was rewarded with a slight nod indicating his approval to confirm what Lumpkin apparently knew and the *Post* suspected. "You mean Captain Ronald Espy?" I said.

"Exactly. If word gets out you're looking at him for that midshipman's death, there'll be a feeding frenzy."

When I looked to Scully this time I got a blank stare, indicating he had sidelined himself. "What's the problem?" I asked Lumpkin. "Just tell 'em we don't discuss on-going investigations."

"It's not that simple," he replied. "They seem to have a pretty reliable source, which means if we don't give them something they'll run with what they have."

I was beginning to think that wasn't such a bad idea, when he said, "Don't let his rank or lack of an official title fool you. Captain Espy's a savvy Pentagon insider and a master at operating beneath the media's radar. If he gets tagged as your primary suspect the shit's gonna fly."

Having heard it all from Scully, Carol and Espy himself, I said, "I know about Force Transformation."

But Lumpkin hadn't finished. "And do you know he was a major player in cancelling the Army's prized multi-billion dollar howitzer, the Crusader? And that he's standing between the Navy and a component of its long-range shipbuilding program, the littoral combat ship?"

From what I had read about the ship's many short-comings, I would have guessed that would endear him to many folks. "No," I had to admit.

"There's more," he said, "but I think you see where I'm going. As a key player on the SecDef's tranforma-tion team, Captain Espy has made some high-level enemies, folks who don't appreciate his role in FT, or his White House connections. So, if it's even hinted that he was involved in any way with this midship-man's death, they'll come after him with daggers. Which means we have to be ready, Agent Shore."

Now, in addition to working this case, and trying to figure out who was targeting Sis, I was about to become the Chief of Information's frontman. "Call me Jerzy," I said, unable to think of anything else at the moment.

Lumpkin looked at me. "*Jerzy* Shore?"

"Uh-huh," I uttered, thinking, with a name like Pickett Lumpkin he'd understand.

Apparently he did, because he nodded and we moved on, which is when I decided I could like this guy.

"So where do we go from here?" I asked, since Scully was no longer part of the discussion.

"Let's put our heads together and come up with something innocuous to tell the *Post*." His confidence, coupled with his easy manner, had me believing he could put a positive spin on the sinking of the Titanic.

"Something that takes the spotlight off Captain Espy?" I offered.

Again, he nodded. "Exactly. But not anything misleading that might bite us in the tail later if he's guilty."

"In other words, something that neither implicates him nor exonerates him?" And when he agreed I thought, too bad. "How do we do that?"

"I suggest characterizing your investigation as routine without singling out anyone. The boy's death has already been ruled an accident and you're merely re-examining the facts. Correct?"

I looked at Scully, and we both nodded. "And why am I doing that?" I asked.

"NCIS received an unsubstantiated claim that raises questions about the initial investigation," Lumpkin went on, "and now you're checking it out by interviewing Resnick's former schoolmates and anyone who may've known him during his brief time at the academy, as well as those involved in the investigation."

"I haven't gotten to some of those yet."

"But you will, right?"

"Yeah," I said, thinking, if the damn elephants would only stop interfering and let me do my job. Meanwhile, I was still miffed at Carol's strident defense of Espy earlier, and that she no doubt alerted him about my passing his name on to Barone. "You're sure you don't want to say he's a suspect?" I asked.

Lumpkin shook his head. "Let's just draw from the foregoing to formulate our response. And while we're at it," he said, removing a notebook from his briefcase, "we'll develop additional background in the form of follow-up Qs and As to draw from should we need it; something that keeps it all in perspective."

By the time I had finished briefing him on where I was in the investigation, and helped craft what we all agreed was an appropriate response to the *Post*'s query, it was late afternoon. We concluded with Lumpkin putting his notebook away, and telling us, "This will do for now. We should plan to work together from here on," he said to Scully. "Meanwhile, good luck with your investigation, Agent Shore."

As I watched him leave, I felt certain I had lost my hold on the case.

Fifteen

"What the hell was that about, Chief?" I asked after Lumpkin left. "How'd the *Post* get word of my investigation, and what's Chinfo's real role in this game?"

"Obviously, someone leaked it to them," he replied with a shrug.

"And Lumpkin?"

Another shrug. "As he said, like it or not, the press is on board. And since we can't ignore 'em, we'll have to rely on Chinfo's PR team to run interference for us."

I shook my head. "I'm beginning to really dislike this case." And when he raised an eyebrow, I said, "We've lost control. That is, if we ever had it."

Scully brushed aside my concerns with a wave. "Don't let this business with the *Post* throw you. Do your job and let me worry about the rest."

I wasn't going to win this battle and, so, taking my cue to leave I rose and headed for the door. "Whatever you say, Chief."

I was still unsettled over the dustup with Carol, and to make up for it I decided to give her a heads-up about the *Washington Post* query and Chinfo's entry into the equation. This time when the master chief put me through I got her recording saying she was either on the phone or away from her desk and to leave a message, which I did—a brief account of our meeting and what Lumpkin intended. That done, I checked back with Agent Joe Ricci in Annapolis to see if he had any luck running down Resnick's roommates through the alumni association.

"I was about to call you," he said. "Got the info on both roomies. One's a retired commander living in Poway, just north of San Diego. Name's Glen Kelly. Works for Scripps Institute of Oceanography in La Jolla commanding one of their research ships, the R/V *Roger Revelle*, currently operating out of Taiwan in the Philippine Sea."

"Wonderful. Just what I need, a trip to the Philippines."

"Relax, Iceman." I could tell he was enjoying himself. "According to the folks at Scripps he's available via satellite and e-mail."

"Okay," I said, calming a bit. "What about the other clown? Where's he, Timbuktu?"

"Much closer. Lieutenant Joseph Koontz is a medically retired Navy SEAL living in Virginia Beach."

I didn't like the sound of that. "What type of medical retirement?" I asked cautiously.

"Got shot up pretty bad in some covert operation," Ricci said.

"Spell it out."

There was a pause. "Shrapnel from an RPG round. He's partially paralyzed and has difficulty speaking. Wish I had better news, my friend."

I jotted down both names and contact info, thanked him and hung up. I checked my watch. It was nearly five, which made it five a.m. in the Philippines; too early to call Kelly. But I couldn't wait, not with Chinfo and the *Post* now in the game. Turning to my computer, I drafted a brief email identifying myself and explaining that I was investigating Jeff Resnick's death. I ended by saying we needed to talk ASAP and asking when he would be available. Then, clicking High Priority, I hit Send, and crossed my fingers.

The good chi must have been flowing. Twenty minutes later my phone rang.

"Kelly here," he said in the way of an introduction. "Can you talk now?"

"Ready when you are," I replied while he assaulted my eardrum with a coughing fit.

"Damn cigarettes," he sputtered. "Whatdya say?"

"I said, ready when you are."

"I'm ready now. Why else would I be calling?" Then, clearing his throat, he asked, "What's this business about Jeff's death? I thought that was behind us."

"It was until someone came forward," I replied, and quickly provided the details of how it began, pausing occasionally while he cleared his lungs.

"So, what do you want from me?"

"I'd like to begin with that night, and what you knew about Resnick's plans for it."

There was a momentary pause. "If you read the report you know I told the investigating officer I was asleep when Jeff sneaked out."

"Look, Commander…,"

"It's lieutenant commander," he corrected me.

"Excuse me. I was informed you'd retired with the rank of commander." And when he laughed, I asked, "What am I missing?"

"What the hell," he said with a sigh. "It doesn't matter anymore. I was booted out. Eighty-sixed. Given early retirement when they discovered I was gay." He went on to explain that he had been selected for commander but, having been outed, was quietly forced to resign before being promoted.

This gave the case a new slant, one I hadn't considered, so I asked, not too delicately, if anyone at the academy knew he'd been gay. He answered with a simple yes, and I asked, "Was Jeff Resnick also gay?"

"What difference would it make? The guy's dead," he said expelling what sounded like a lungful of sputum.

"I don't pretend to know the inner workings of life at the academy," I replied, "but it certainly might be a factor if he was."

"Well, he wasn't. We would've known."

"*We?* You saying you weren't the only one?"

"Aren't you clever. That's exactly what I'm saying."

"How many?" I asked, intrigued now.

"Surprised?" he said through a phlegmatic laugh.

"Frankly, yes."

"There were enough of us," is all he would say.

"Did your straight classmates know?"

"Don't be ridiculous."

We were straying, but I couldn't resist. "So, did you guys have a secret handshake?"

"Look, Shore," he snapped, "I didn't call to discuss my sex life. I got a twelve-hour workday ahead of me." Then, more calmly, he conceded, "We could usually tell who leaned our way, and we were discrete about how we dealt with it."

"*Usually*? So it's possible Resnick was gay and you and your frien... you didn't pick up on it during the short time you were roommates."

"I think I would've known," he assured me.

"Could he have been a switch hitter?"

"How the hell would I know! Anything's possible. But he wasn't one of us. Okay?"

"Okay," I said, moving on. "Did you know he was going to Mahan Hall that night to hang the banner?"

I could easily imagine Kelly sucking on a cigarette as he thought back. After a moment I heard him exhale, and he said, "I remember when we were in our room that night Jeff was called out, and when he returned he was hyped about something. I didn't give it much thought. There were a lot of crazy things going on that week."

"Hyped about what? Did he say?"

"Uh-uh. Just kept to himself. Maybe hyped is the wrong word. He was more animated than usual. But it wasn't anything we discussed."

"Did you know he kept a journal?"

"Yeah. I think quite a few plebes did that first year. Some were more conscientious about it than others. I know he was."

"Did you ever take a quick peek?"

"You're a piece of work, Shore. No, I didn't take a peek, quick or otherwise. I wasn't interested. Besides, who had time? They kept us running."

"Who kept you running?"

"The upperclassmen. Between academics and life in Mother Bancroft we barely had enough energy to crawl into our racks at the end of the day."

"How about after he fell from the tower? Might you have looked through it then?"

"You're like a goddamn pit bull."

"Please answer the question." And when he repeated that he hadn't, I said, "I'm asking, because several pages are missing—removed with a razor or X-Acto knife—so their absence wouldn't be noted. You sure you didn't go through it?"

"Answer's still no. Besides, I couldn't have if I wanted to."

"Why not?"

"Because Jeff's belongings, including his journal, were boxed up by our company officer the next day and taken away."

"Taken where?"

"To the commandant, I think."

"You mean Briggs? Captain Winthrop Briggs?"

"Yeah."

"And you never saw them again?"

"Correct."

"What else can you tell me about the events surrounding Jeff's death?"

He clicked his tongue, and said, "There was the funeral service, where I spoke with his parents. That was terribly sad. His mother wanting to know if Jeff was happy. And, did he have many friends. That sort of stuff. His father, being an alumnus, seemed to understand more than his wife, but you could see he was hurting too. Then there was the accident investigation. We were asked what, if anything, we knew about Jeff going to the tower. I don't recall anyone knew anything. We were all in shock."

"Prior to the interview were you prompted in any way to say something you might not otherwise say, or asked to forget certain facts or events leading up to Jeff's death?"

"By whom?"

I didn't like leading him, but I needed to know. "By upperclassmen," I said.

"No."

"Were you and Joseph Koontz interviewed together?" I asked.

"Now there's a name out of the past. Poor Joe. I guess you know about him."

"Yes," I said, and listened while he reminisced.

"Joe was something," he said with sadness. "Came to the academy from some dirt-poor west Texas town for one reason only, to be a Navy SEAL. I remember him telling us how in high school he had been torn between entering the priesthood and the SEALs, and that once he'd decided, nothing and no one was going to get in his way. He was quite remarkable."

"What about the interview?" I asked, pulling him back.

He paused. "We were interviewed separately. It was brief and informal. The investigating officer asking if I had prior knowledge of Jeff's plan that night, and if I'd been involved in any way. And when I said no, she asked if I knew of anyone who may've been involved. Again, I said I didn't, and that the first I'd heard about it was when we learned of the accident at quarters that morning. From what Joe told me later, he pretty much said the same."

"So you don't believe he was prompted to alter his testimony either?"

"No way. Anyone who knows Joe knows he would never lie."

"But you did," I said.

"I just told you I didn't."

"I mean about being gay. At the time, before don't ask, don't tell, you weren't supposed to be there if you were gay. So you lied."

"That was different." Then, his voice dropping, he said quietly, in a way that had me thinking he truly missed the Navy, "They've corrected that now."

It was time to shift gears again, and I asked, "Do you recall Midshipman Second Class Carol Rutter?"

"Sure," he said rebounding with a cheerful laugh.

"Did I say something funny?" I asked, feeling my pulse quicken.

"No. It's just that everyone in the brigade knew Rutter. She was a head-turner."

"What about your…"

"…my preferences?"

"I didn't think you would've…"

"…noticed her?"

I didn't like him completing my sentences. "…found her attractive," I said.

"I didn't. But being gay doesn't mean you don't admire a pretty woman. Besides, she was a lovely person, so unlike the other upperclassmen. And, while I wasn't interested, I appreciated her empathy for us. As far as finding her attractive, many plebes did, including Jeff. And, for whatever reason she chose to mentor him."

"And how did that go?" I asked.

"Okay, I guess. At least initially. Then things changed around early November when she stopped having him come around. When I asked about it, he said it was because she was busy preparing for mid-terms. It seemed to bother him for a time, but that didn't last long. Plebes didn't have time to dwell on trivialities."

"Anything else about her that you recall?"

"I thought this is about Jeff."

"I'm interested in anyone who knew him. What about Midshipman First Class Ron Espy? Did you know him?"

"Of course. He was brigade commander. But what's he got to do with Jeff's death?"

"I'm not saying he does."

"You're asking. So there must be some connection."

"Did Espy have any dealings with Resnick?"

He replied immediately. "You must be joking. I'd be surprised if he knew any of us existed. He was in the stratosphere and we were in the trenches."

We talked a while longer, but there was nothing more he could add to what he had already told me, and so I thanked him and asked if I might contact him again if necessary. He began another coughing spell, and managed to say I could before hanging up.

Sixteen

I pushed away from my desk, leaned back and gazed out at the darkening sky, my thoughts in a jumble as I considered scenarios that had a gay plebe and a high-ranking midshipman in a relationship that resulted in one of them being killed. The problem with that premise, though, was that I felt Kelly would surely have known if his roommate were gay. What was it he said? *We could usually tell who leaned our way.* Yet, there were factors I couldn't discount, such as the missing journal pages, and Espy's interest in Resnick, a lowly, insignificant plebe. Then, too, there was the photo of a slight, delicate-looking youth I saw back at the Resnick's. In the end, unable to discount the possibility of a liaison between them, I put the gay scenario aside to let it percolate.

I arrived at Carol's precisely at nine with my peace offering, a bouquet of colorful spring flowers and a pepperoni pizza.

"Jerzy! What a lovely surprise," she said pressing the flowers to her nose. "They're beautiful." She was still in uniform, and hadn't yet noticed the pizza. That is, till I stepped inside and the aroma quickly overtook the gentler fragrance of the flowers. Then, peering over them, she glimpsed down and laughed. "You're a hoot, Agent Shore." Unlike this afternoon, her mood was light, almost childlike.

Pleased with the change, I followed her to the kitchen, where she quickly found a vase and filled it with water, all the while chattering about adoring freshly cut flowers and never having enough free time to enjoy them. Once she had carefully arranged them, trimming leaves and clipping stems, she turned and came to me, throwing her arms around my neck. "For the flowers," she said, and kissed me. "And this one's for being so thoughtful," she added, nodding at the pizza. Then, pulling away, she announced that she was famished, and would I grab a bottle of wine from the cupboard while she changed.

"No need to," I said, not wanting her out of sight for a second. "You look terrific."

She winked and patted my cheek. "You're a sweetheart. Be right back." And she was gone.

I chose a bottle of Cotes du Rhone from among several French reds, popped the cork and set the kitchen table. I could hear her moving upstairs as I poured out two glasses. Minutes later she was bouncing barefooted downstairs in snug jeans and a blue polo shirt, sans bra.

We ate quickly, with little conversation, devouring the pie and consuming most of the wine. Later, we settled in the living room, she at one end of the sofa, me at the opposite end cradling her feet in my lap.

"Relaxed?" I asked as I pressed my thumbs into her soles.

"Completely," she purred with a tired smile. "Could you do this, say, once a week?"

"I'll think about it," I said.

"No need to bring flowers or pizza, but they would be appreciated." Then, with a devilish grin, "I promise to make it worthwhile."

"You're on." Our eyes met and I said, "Should we take this conversation upstairs?"

"Tempting," she replied. Then, pulling herself up and tucking her legs beneath her, she said, "How's the case going?"

Trying not to show disappointment, I shrugged and said, "Moving along. But I'm no longer certain in what direction." Then, noting her frown, I told her of my conversation with Lieutenant Commander Glen Kelly.

"You're joking!" she said when I mentioned the academy's gay contingent.

"You didn't know?"

"I had no idea. I wonder how many."

"He didn't say, but I sensed it was a goodly number."

She laughed. "That would explain... "

"Explain what?"

"Nothing really. I was thinking about a classmate."

"An unresponsive classmate?"

"Sorta. It didn't make sense then."

"But it does now."

She replied with a slight nod.

I decided there was no point withholding my earlier thoughts concerning Resnick and Espy. So, I asked, "Could Resnick have been gay?"

"Is that what Kelly told you?"

"He said he didn't know. But I've seen his photograph, and, frankly, I thought he looked somewhat—"

"Fragile?" And when I nodded, she said, "Jeff wasn't gay."

"You seem certain."

"I am," is all she'd say, which left me wondering if there might have been more to their relationship than mentoring.

Before heading down that road, though, I asked, "Might've he been a switch-hitter?"

"I suppose anything's possible," she conceded.

"What about Espy?"

"Where are you going with this?"

"I'm looking for a motive."

"This is bizarre."

"I've worked stranger cases," I replied.

She continued shaking her head as I laid it out for her. "Suppose Espy was, or is, bi-sexual."

"That's ridiculous."

"Let's just suppose," I insisted. "And let's also assume for the moment he didn't realize he had those leanings, that is, until he encountered someone who aroused them. Now, just put yourself in his place, and imagine what might be going though his mind. Nothing like this has happened before. You're terribly conflicted and don't know how to deal with it. You certainly can't confide in anyone, not without risking ridicule or, worse, expulsion. Your first response has to be denial. Yet, the more you suppress these yearnings, the stronger they become. Then, to further complicate matters, the girl you dated…" I nearly said, "and slept with," but caught myself. "…is mentoring the boy you're suddenly attracted to." I paused, allowing the image to set in. After a moment, I asked, "What sort of thoughts—no, passions—might've simmered beneath the surface back then in Bancroft Hall, and what emotions might they kindle, particularly whenever Espy saw the two of you together?"

She sat motionless, no longer protesting, her eyes fixed on mine.

"Then one day there's a serendipitous encounter—perhaps in the gym, or locker room, or pool, it doesn't matter where," I said. "What matters, though, is for the first time they're alone—the plebe and the omnipotent brigade commander and Green Bowler—and in that moment Espy, who never considered doing anything like this, makes an inappropriate comment or move. One can only imagine what happens next."

Carol swallowed hard. "Go on."

"Well, you have to wonder how Resnick responds. Does he submit? And, if he does, is it because he's so inclined, or because he fears reprisal if he doesn't. But if he's straight, as you say, what then? Does he have the fortitude to rebuff a ranking upperclassman's advances?" When I paused this time, she leaned forward, as if expecting the answer. Instead, I said, "An interesting scenario, wouldn't you say?"

But she didn't say. And when she replied, she heaved a sigh and said, "This is insane."

"It may be, but when you take Resnick's journal into account it becomes plausible."

"His journal? You got all that from Jeff's journal?"

I didn't want to lie. "No, there's nothing there suggesting it." And when she knitted her brow, I explained, "Rather, it's what's missing from the journal that interests me."

"I don't understand," she said.

"The pages containing Resnick's final entries were removed—surgically removed, so as to make the book appear whole. You have to wonder why someone would do that instead of simply tearing them out."

"And you think Ron did it to protect himself? That's quite a leap."

I shook my head. "Espy didn't remove them. I doubt he even knew what Resnick had written. Nor did he have access to it. The journal, along with the rest of Resnick's belongings, was removed from his room soon after he died and delivered to the commandant, Captain Briggs."

"You think Briggs read it and removed them?"

I nodded. "He was protecting Espy, a fellow Green Bowler, just as he did during the investigation."

Again, she leaned forward. "Do you have the pages?"

"They're gone. No doubt destroyed."

"So, you really don't know what Jeff wrote," she said, settling back again.

"True. But I'm betting it had to do with Espy."

"About Ron being gay?"

"That's one possibility."

She rubbed her chin. "But why strike out at Jeff? Why not me? After all, I was the one who reached out to him."

I shook my head. "I can't see Espy harming the person who validated his masculinity, certainly not if he was questioning it. Whereas, taking the boy out of the picture resolved several nagging issues."

"Such as...."

"Without Resnick there was no one whose testimony could expel him if, in fact, he made a play for the boy, or forced himself on him against his will. Further, absent the source of his arousal, it would be easier to suppress his erotic feelings and carry on as before. Then, too, there's the jealousy factor."

"This is all fascinating," she said. "Not very believable, but quite fascinating."

But I wasn't through. It was time to ask what had been troubling me since talking with Kelly. "Why'd you stop having Resnick come around?"

The question seemed to surprise her, and she looked away for a moment. Then, frowning, she said, "It was cruel, I know. It hurt him." And when I didn't comment, she said, "You think we were having an affair, don't you?"

I had dismissed that notion earlier. "No, I don't. I suspect your motives were pure, that your only interest was helping him. As for Resnick, I think he saw you as an anchor to windward in a turbulent sea. From what I've determined, plebe year is pretty tough. They're either harassed or being ignored, and rarely do upper-classmen extend a kind hand, as you did. So I'm sure he valued your support. Even Kelly noted how much he and the others appreciated your empathy for them."

"I'm sure they did. I was fortunate to have a mentor when I was a plebe, and it made a difference."

"And your reason for cutting Resnick off?"

"It was Ron. You were right about his jealousy. He made it clear he didn't approve. Not that I cared what he thought," she quickly added. "We were no longer dating. But I was concerned for Jeff."

"Concerned, how?"

"Not for his safety, if that's what you're thinking. I didn't want him harassed more than necessary. Between life in Bancroft, academics, and extracurricular activities, he didn't need the added burden of Ron and his pals riding him. Jeff was bright and motivated. Given the chance he would make it through, so, for his sake, I backed off."

"Knowing Espy as I do, I'd say that was the right decision," I said.

She opened her mouth, and I sensed she was about to say, "You don't know him at all." Instead, she hesitated, and said, "It's late."

My cue to leave. In light of the day's events, I thought it best not to push it. "Time flies when I'm with you," I said as I stood.

To my surprise, she leaned over, tugged my sleeve, and whispered, "Don't go."

Seventeen

The bedspread had been thrown back when I stepped from the adjoining bathroom, and Carol was stretched atop the sheets on her side, one hand propping up her head, the other resting casually across her breasts. Her jeans and shirt were on the chair, and the lamp was off, leaving the room in the soft glow of the streetlight. She had raised the window, and a gentle river breeze now fluttered the curtains. I had never been in the room before, yet I felt momentarily unsettled by the familiarity of the scene. And as I crossed to her, I realized it was Carol. She was wearing the same mischievous smile I had come to know so well from her photo. In the next instant I was beside her, lost in her embrace.

Her invitation to stay had thrown me, and I nearly talked myself out of it when I foolishly asked about her needing to be up early for work. Then, for an agonizing instant, I mentally kicked myself as I watched her consider the question before saying it wouldn't be a problem.

Our love-making began tentatively, with me offering soft carefully placed kisses and long caresses, until she took the lead, and then it exploded. She was far less inhibited and, I might add, more vigorous than I, making me realize my life lacked more than mere female companionship. It lacked the imagination and verve of youth. Afterward, while lying beside her, I was certain any doubts about merging my personal life with this case were insignificant. I was in love, and I told her so before drifting off.

It seemed I had just closed my eyes when I heard the alarm. The digital clock beside the bed read 5:00. I reached over in the darkness, and found her space still warm.

From across the room, she whispered, "Go back to sleep. I'll wake you when the coffee's ready."

I glimpsed her shadow and suggested she return to bed, but got no response. After a moment I heard the shower and I grew aroused picturing her lathering herself. When next I awoke she was standing beside me in full uniform holding a steaming mug of coffee.

"Rise and shine," she said, causing me to force one eye open.

"It's Saturday," I protested.

"You have a lot to learn about the Navy," she said, setting the cup beside the bed. "Time to hit the deck."

I ran a hand over my face and blinked her into focus. "God, you're beautiful."

She smiled and headed for the door. "See you downstairs."

The *Washington Post* was on the kitchen table, open to a brief article disclosing NCIS's investigation into

Resnick's accidental death, and saying little else. I noted only two names, mine and a Lieutenant Kenneth Burgess, identified as a Navy Pentagon spokesman. Lumpkin had managed to keep Espy's name out of it.

"Looks benign enough," she said with a nod at the paper.

"I guess we have Captain Lumpkin to thank for that," I replied. Then, noting her expression, I asked, "What's wrong?"

"I'll have to call him as soon as I get in. Find out what's coming next."

"What could be next? This pretty much says it all without mentioning our boy Espy."

"We'll see," she said before checking her watch. "We better get moving. It's late."

"It's only five thirty," I said, not wanting our time together to end.

"And I have to be at my desk by six."

As we headed for the door, I said confidently, "What time will I see you tonight?"

She paused, and I could tell from her expression that what she was about to say wasn't what I wanted to hear. "It's probably a good idea if we pass tonight." Then noting my disappointment, she added, "Jerzy, this is moving very quickly for me. I need time to make sense of it." And when I frowned, she leaned in and said, "Please try to understand."

She was right, of course. Yet, standing there with her in the shadows, I yearned to know she felt as I did. If she needed time to figure it out, so be it. I nodded, and we parted with a hasty kiss, while I consoled myself with the notion that we all move at different paces.

* * *

The sun was still down when I arrived home. My newspaper was on the lawn, its plastic sleeve dripping dew. I picked it up, shook it, and gazed at the headline through the sleeve while wondering what more Carol expected to learn from Lumpkin.

The instant I entered the house I sensed something wasn't right, and I paused in the entryway, my hand frozen on the light switch. The house was dark and I wanted to keep it that way until I figured out what was happening. My senses were on high alert as I pressed against the wall, straining to listen. There were no sounds beyond my own shallow breathing— no movement anywhere, not a masked footstep or the creak of a floorboard. Yet, certain I wasn't alone, I drew my revolver and stood motionless waiting for the approaching dawn.

As dark yielded to gray twilight I made out familiar shapes; the staircase ahead of me and the chairs and coffee table in the living room, but nothing out of the ordinary. Then it hit me, the house was too quiet. I wasn't hearing the steady hum of the aerator from the aquarium in the next room. I thought perhaps a power failure, an increasingly frequent occurrence during storms. But the weather had been fair. When I could see well enough, I slipped into the living room, sweeping my gun before me. There was no one, and I moved back to the den, where the fish tank had been smashed.

All but a few remaining inches of water had spilled onto the carpet along with my nine now-dead fish. A brass bookend in the shape of an anchor, one of two from the bookshelf, lay at the bottom of the tank.

I sidestepped the mess, my heel squishing against the rug, and began searching the rest of the house and adjoining garage, but there was no one and no other damage, except the jimmied back door where the intruder had entered. Nor was anything missing, which is what I told Detective Barone when he showed up shortly after the Arlington police cruiser responded to my call.

"You sure nothing was stolen?" he asked as we stood in the den. He was still chewing the stub of an unlit cigar, and I wondered if it was the same one.

"Doesn't appear to be."

"And what about this?" he said pointing to the note on the desk. "Did you touch it?"

I shook my head. "Course not. I haven't touched a thing. I saved that for your boys."

Barone looked down at the tightly scrawled letters—*YOU'RE GONNA PAYYOU BASTARD*—and asked, "What do you make of it?"

"It could mean Espy's getting anxious."

"Why now?"

"The *Post*'s interest in the case and the piece in today's edition," I said. "It might've set him off."

"I didn't see it. What's it say?"

I showed him. "No suspects mentioned. Just that there's an investigation into the death of the midshipman."

"You think he read it this morning and ran over here and attacked your fish?" His deadpan expression and tone suggesting either I was an idiot or thought he was.

"No. But I'm sure he knew about the query before the article appeared."

It was clear he wasn't buying that either, and he asked, "Got any other theories?"

"Could be that Joe fella."

Barone removed his cigar, studied it, and shoved it in his pocket. "Lemme see if I got this straight," he said. "You got home around six?" And when I nodded, he smirked and said, "You NCIS guys put in long hours."

I didn't feel the need to explain where I'd been and with whom. "It's a tough job," I said.

He grunted. "Yeah, tough. The house alarmed?" And when I said it was, he asked why I hadn't turned it on.

I thought about how I had rushed home from Whole Foods with the flowers, showered, dressed and had the pizza delivered before dashing out again with my arms loaded. "I left in a rush."

"Do that often?"

"Go out in a rush?"

"You know what I mean."

I shrugged. "Sometimes. If I'm running to the Safeway and coming right back I won't turn it on."

"Zat where you were headed last night, the Safeway?" he said, his eyes floating over my jacket and tie.

"I had other business."

"With the case?"

"I do have a personal life," I answered, noticing his wedding band for the first time.

"Must be nice," he said.

Meanwhile, the forensic team was wrapping up. They had dusted for prints and checked the point of entry, as well as the yard and path along the side of the house, photographing it all. Before leaving, the team leader asked Barone if he could take the note. They would check it for prints as well. I sensed there wouldn't be any, mainly because whoever wrote it was astute enough to take the gold Cross pen I kept beside the notepad.

I phoned Scully at home after everyone had left and was told he'd gone to the office. When I reached him, I briefed him on what had happened. He, too, doubted Espy was involved, but wasn't ready to eliminate him either. Next, I cleaned up as best I could, gathering the fish and giving them a water funeral down the toilet, and rolling up the rug and tossing it over the back fence to dry.

It wasn't until nine before I left the house. The forensic van was still outside, the team dispersed throughout the neighborhood interviewing anyone who might have seen or heard anything. By the time I reached the office, Scully had summoned Theo, our resident forensic specialist and, together, they were going over my old cases.

"Looking for a suspect," Scully said, when I asked what was going on. "Someone who might want revenge," he explained. "You've racked up some impressive convictions, and any one of those bozos, or their friends, could be after you. If there's a lead Theo will find it," he assured me.

"Sure thing, Iceman," Theo agreed.

"Meanwhile, watch your back," Scully warned. And with that bit of advice, he handed me the names of the officer who investigated Resnick's death and the JAG officer who reviewed the accident report. "Got these from Navy Personnel. Probably won't get much from either of `em, but see what you come up with."

Theo and I left together and headed downstairs, where I apologized for lousing up his weekend.

He laughed it off. "One of the disadvantages of bachelorhood." As I headed for my office, he called, "You think of anything, give me a holler."

"Will do," I said, and moved on.

Someone had invaded my world twice now, and I didn't like it. Fortunately, the guy wasn't a pro, of that I was certain. A pro would have studied my movements and, knowing I wasn't home, returned when I was. And he certainly wouldn't have left a calling card, as this clown had, which told me this guy had been improvising, and then acted out of anger or frustration at not finding me there. He was playing out of his league, and that was a plus for me. Still, that he'd tracked down both me and my sister, told me he was determined. And, as I reminded myself, amateurs do get lucky sometimes, which is why I would have to rely on Theo and Barone to do their part.

I had read the accident report and saw that it followed the Navy's procedure for an accidental death— a one-officer investigation coordinated with NCIS, reviewed by the academy's Staff Judge Advocate, and forwarded up the chain of command to the Judge Advocate General. In this instance, the Commandant of Midshipmen had appointed Lieutenant Commander Sandra Rose, a brigade officer, to conduct the investigation and write the report. The lawyer reviewing her work was Commander Charles Ford.

Of the two, I began with Rose since she was closest to the events. According to Scully, her name was now Bookwalter, and she resided in Madison, Connecticut. I figured she was about my age, judging by her rank at the time. As I punched in her number I hoped she had a clear memory of the incident.

The phone rang for some time before she picked it up, and I could imagine her rushing in from her car with an armful of groceries.

"Hello," she said slightly winded. Her voice reminded me of a drill sergeant's.

I immediately identified myself, explaining simply that I was reviewing the circumstances surrounding Resnick's death, and asking if she could spare a few minutes. She said she could, and I proceeded to review her role in the investigation.

"Yes," she confirmed, "I was appointed by the commandant, Captain Briggs."

"Was there a reason why he selected you?"

"If there was, I wasn't aware of it. It was a collateral duty assignment, and I figured it was my turn. I remember telling him at the time that I'd never conducted an investigation, and he told me not to worry, that it was straightforward, and to come to him if I had questions."

"And did you have questions or problems?"

"None that I recall. It was sad, of course. The boy's death. But I gathered the facts, wrote them up, and passed them on to Briggs."

"What else did you pass on to him?" I asked.

"I don't follow you."

"You collected Midshipman Resnick's belongings."

"Oh, yes. They'd been packed up by his company officer, and I delivered them as well."

"Without first going through them?"

She thought a moment. "I don't recall, but I must have. There was an inventory sheet, and I would not have turned them over without verifying it was correct."

I had the inventory sheet with her signature in front of me, so I figured she was telling the truth.

"Do you recall seeing his journal among his belongings?"

There was another pause. "Agent Shore, that was decades ago. Why do you ask?"

She sounded genuinely puzzled, and so I told her about the missing pages, and the possibility they contained information pertinent to Resnick's death, which seemed to surprise her.

"You're making it sound as though it wasn't an accident. Is that why you're looking into it?"

It was time to bring in the anonymous letter.

"You surely don't think I removed them," she said, her voice rising with each word. I could easily imagine her back stiffening.

"Someone did."

"Well, *I* certainly didn't."

"And you didn't notice they were missing when you inventoried his belongings?"

"That would've required reading the journal, and I didn't do that."

"Why not?"

"I suppose I didn't think it was necessary." She was getting agitated.

"That's too bad. Do you recall the interviews you conducted with young Resnick's classmates?"

"Yes," she said, guardedly now, and then began ticking them off. "There were the boy's roommates, his circle of friends, his company officer, and the maintenance crew at Mahan Hall. Oh, yes, and the duty officer who found him. There weren't that many."

"Did you discuss that list with Captain Briggs?"

"I may have. I was giving him progress reports."

"At his request?"

"Yes."

"And did he guide you along the way?"

"Possibly. I don't recall."

At this point, I was pretty sure he did. "I'm wondering why you didn't interview Midshipman Ronald Espy."

"Espy?" She paused a moment. "He was the brigade commander. Why on earth would I do that?"

"Why wouldn't you?"

"Because I interviewed only those directly connected to the boy."

I let that slide for the moment, and asked, "Did you determine who, if anyone, had put Resnick up to the prank?"

"Everything is in the report, Agent Shore. As you will note, I concluded that he obtained the banner from some upperclassmen and later decided to hang it from the clock tower atop Mahan Hall."

"Yes, I saw that you spoke to the mids who gave him the banner—Ted Benson and Larry Smith—and you noted they thought he intended hanging it from his window in Bancroft Hall, as other mids were doing that week."

"That's right. Since no one I spoke with knew of any plan to display it from the tower, I concluded it had been his decision alone. Have you learned something to the contrary? Is that what the letter said?"

"I'm not at liberty to say what I've learned, Commander."

"You mentioned Midshipman Espy. Do you suspect he may've been involved somehow?"

"I can't speculate on what we—"

"Now you listen to me, Agent Shore! I was tasked to look into an accidental death, and on that basis there was no reason to speculate otherwise, or to expand my investigation beyond that point. So I strongly resent any implication that my investigation and my report are in any way lacking. Do you read me?" she said with precision.

I hadn't intended our discussion to escalate into a row, which was where most seemed to go lately, and I quickly assured her, "It's not my intention to discredit your work. To the contrary, I'm certain you did as you were instructed. My concern, given the letter we received, is to determine if you had been directed away from information that may've caused you to conclude otherwise."

There was a momentary pause, and she replied more calmly, "The only direction I received—which was minimal—was from the commandant, Captain Briggs. So, if what you're insinuating is true, then I was misdirected by him." Again, her tone suggested that possibility was unlikely. "Perhaps you should be asking him," she concluded.

"I can't. He's dead."

"Oh, I didn't know."

I ended our conversation in the standard way, asking if I might contact her again should I have additional questions. She consented, but reluctantly. When I hung up I was sure it was Briggs who removed the pages from Resnick's journal.

It wasn't until late afternoon that I was able to track down now-retired Captain Ford, the JAG officer who reviewed Bookwalter's report. And when I did, he had little to say beyond confirming he had run a legal eye over it before forwarding it on.

The day was ending strangely for me. I was heading out the door knowing some nut was hunting for me, and no concrete leads to go on. Meanwhile, I was lost in the memory of my evening with Carol, and troubled by her need to sort things out. Should I not have said I loved her? Well, I had, and I was glad of it. If our relationship was to blossom, she needed to know it. Yet, something deep down told me I may have erred.

* * *

I was back from Sis' around seven thirty, and while I wasn't very hungry, I fried two pork chops and served them with steamed broccoli. Afterward, determined to put all thoughts of Carol, the Resnick case, and the intruder out of my head, I settled back with a new Donald Westlake mystery and two fingers of Dalwhinnie Scotch. A half hour later, having refilled my glass and downing it, I was still on page one and no closer to emptying my brain than when I had started. That's when I decided to put the booze aside and get a dose of night air.

I drove through Arlington's Clarendon district, past rows of busy restaurants, aimlessly heading toward Alexandria, where it seemed every sidewalk table in Old Town was occupied. Soon I was driving past Carol's, where I parked after circling the block several times. It was nearly ten and her lights were on, and for a moment I toyed with the notion of knocking on her door.

"Hi. I just happened to be in the neighborhood and saw your lights, and wondered if you could use some company." And when she said, no, what then? On the other hand, she might welcome me in. My thoughts tumbled on like that until I spotted a shadowed figure approach her door. I strained to make him out, but couldn't. And when she opened it and he stepped inside all hope vanished.

I sat there wanting to believe he was from her office. I thought of those absurdly long working hours, her goal of reaching flag rank, even of her whispered conversation with the four-star in the hall, and concluded whoever it was had to be there on Navy business, but I couldn't leave without knowing for sure. And so I sat there in the dark and waited. It was well past eleven when I snapped awake. I had no idea when I had nodded off, only that her windows were darkened and I was cold and stiff.

I entered my house with my gun out and, after shutting off the alarm, repeated my earlier routine of checking each room and closet, as well as the attic and basement. It was after midnight when I finally climbed into bed, vowing to replace the aquarium the next day, but it wasn't till dawn that I fell asleep.

Eighteen

Monday passed without incident. For the most part, my telephone and email sat idle. There were no calls from Scully directing me to interview someone. Nothing either from Carol, Lumpkin, or Barone. I had been on a merry-go-round for the past week, and now the world seemed suddenly to have stopped.

By Tuesday I was climbing the walls. With little else to do, I dropped by Theo's after lunch, but he hadn't found anything yet. After reviewing my notes on the Resnick case, I packed away some old files and rearranged my trophy corner. Next, I phoned agent Ricci in Annapolis and told him I wanted to visit the tower that night. I asked if he would arrange it, and he opined that it was a needless exercise, but if I was as bored as I sounded he'd see what he could do. Twenty minutes later he was back, telling me it was all set and to check in with the duty officer when I arrived. I asked if he cared to accompany me and he laughed.

It was close to midnight when I drove down King George Street and pulled up to Gate 1, showed the guard my ID, and asked him to call the duty officer. He directed me to park beside Halsey Field House. The yard was quiet, and except for a few lights in Bancroft Hall, the massive dormitory was dark. Several minutes later, a black Navy car pulled in behind me.

"Good evening. I'm Commander Fetrow," the duty officer said when he came over. "So you want to visit the clock tower." If he thought the idea foolish, particularly at that hour, he didn't say, nor did he appear to think it.

"Yes, I do." With Ricci having cleared it with the Supe's office, I figured he knew why, so there was no need to explain.

"Okay. Follow me."

He returned to his car and led me across the yard, past the Supe's quarters in Buchanan House and the chapel astride the sprawling quadrangle. We circled Sampson Hall and parked behind Mahan Hall, where we entered through a side door. After switching on the lights, he took me up a wide marble staircase and through what had once been the library, where the only sound was the echo of our footsteps.

"In here," he said when we reached a fire door. Then, pushing it open, he switched on the light and pointed up. "Just keep climbing. You expect to be long?"

"I don't think so," I replied.

"Shall I come with you?" he asked.

I shook my head. "No need to."

"Here's the key then. I'll wait here."

I stepped into the stairwell and let the door close behind me. The air was stale and dry. Several cigarette butts littered the landing. I took a few steps and brushed aside a cobweb. Beyond the first landing, the stairs were evenly coated with a dusting of plaster, suggesting no one had come that way for a while. As I climbed, I envisioned a nervous Resnick two-stepping his way to the top with his banner after lights out on that cold November night, propelled by the excitement of his mission, yet fearful of being detected.

The key Commander Fetrow provided was to a heavy brass Yale lock looped through a thick steel hasp, no doubt installed after Resnick's death. The original sliding deadbolt, likely intended to keep the door from blowing open, was still in place, but would have been useless in preventing access to the balcony. I undid both, stepped out onto the narrow landing, and immediately drew back. From ground level, the tower hadn't appeared very high, nor did the balustrade seem as low; it was well below my waist. Combined, the effect was an instant case of rubber legs that had me rethinking why I thought I needed to be there.

I had studied the photos in the accident report, and knew where Resnick had tied off the sheet before the other end had somehow wrapped itself around his neck. Now, looking over the scene, it was obvious two mids working together could easily have done the job and been gone within minutes, which left me wondering why Resnick had come alone. And if he wasn't alone, which I suspected, whoever had helped him gain entry likely remained below—where Fetrow was—as lookout. To my mind, that same someone initiated the prank and assigned it to Resnick.

I was growing accustomed to the height and no longer felt the need to rush off. After a few deep breaths, I moved to the edge and gazed out across the idled campus as Resnick must have—at the chapel dome set against the quiet town, the darkened classrooms, and flowing Severn River—thinking how he must have relished that rare taste of tranquility, which surely eluded him during those hectic plebe days.

In her investigation, Bookwalter concluded that Resnick had sneaked out of Bancroft sometime after one a.m. And while the yard would have looked much as it did now, it must have appeared intimidating to the trespassing midshipman. She had also reported the night had been cold and moonless, with gusts to thirty knots. Definitely a hostile environment, I thought, and no place to be alone. And as I made my way back down, I grew angry thinking that whoever sent him up there must have considered that.

"Well, that was quick," Commander Fetrow said when I returned and handed him the key. "Did you bolt and lock it?"

I assured him I had, and we retraced our route through the empty corridors. He escorted me back to the main gate and, while I left knowing little more than before I arrived, I was more certain Resnick hadn't been acting alone. Proving it, however, was another matter.

As it turned out, I didn't have to. Wednesday's *Washington Post* did it for me, well, at least partially. There in bold letters on the front page below the fold, was the headline, "**Probe focuses on top Pentagon aide**". And beneath it, "Defense official suspect in death of midshipman."

With my coffee cup poised in midair, I read:

Navy investigators are looking into the decades-old accidental death of Naval Academy Midshipman Jeffery Resnick, of Severna Park, Maryland, a freshman, who fell from the school clock tower while attempting to hang a BEAT ARMY banner prior to the annual football contest.

The Naval Criminal Investigative Service reopened the case after the boy's father, Joel Resnick, came forward with an anonymous letter questioning the school's initial findings that his son had acted alone. Information revealed to the Post indicates the NCIS believes Resnick had been ordered to perform the prank by an upperclassman, who then accompanied him into the tower and stood by when the youth fell.

That individual, according to sources, was Brigade Commander Ronald Espy, who is currently serving as special assistant to the Director, Force Transformation, the controversial presidential initiative aimed at restructuring all three military branches.

Telephone calls to Captain Espy and the Resnick household were not returned. Meanwhile, queries directed to the office of the Secretary of Defense have been referred to the Navy, whose spokesman, Captain Pickett Lumpkin, would neither confirm nor deny the allegations. When asked if an indictment is pending, he declined to comment.

I stopped reading when the article shifted to the long-range impact Force Transformation was projected to have on readiness levels and the counter-arguments opposing the initiative. By then it was nearly six thirty, time enough for Carol to be at her desk. I was certain someone in her circle had to be the source of the leak, but would she tell me? I phoned and was told by the master chief that she was out of town until Friday. I thanked him and immediately called Scully.

"Chief," I nearly shouted, "did you see the morning paper!"

"Yeah," he said without enthusiasm.

This wasn't the Scully I knew, and, toning down my own distress, I asked more calmly, "Can you tell me what's going on?"

He replied by asking, "Where are you?"

"Home."

"See me as soon as you get here," is all he said.

"But—"

"We'll talk when you get in," he said, and hung up.

"I'm on my way," I said into the dead phone.

Minutes later I was in my car sorting through a thousand thoughts of Espy and his precious insulated world. Knowing it had just crumbled, I smiled as I envisioned him on the carpet before the Secretary of Defense explaining his side of the story. How I wished I could be there as the bastard tried talking his way out of this mess.

I arrived at Scully's before Miss Happy Face and, seeing his door ajar knocked and entered. He was at his desk rubbing his temples, the *Post* spread out before him. When he looked up with those red eyes I knew he'd been dealing with the story earlier than I had.

"G'morning, Chief," I said tentatively.

"Don't know how good it is," he replied.

"Any idea what's going on?"

"Not much more than what's here," he said, nodding at the paper.

"What about the elephants, have you heard from them?"

"I suspect the herd's being thinned out as we speak."

"Not a word from anyone?"

He frowned and shook his head. "I shoulda heard from the CNO's office by now. It's weird."

"What about Lumpkin?"

He nodded. "We spoke an hour ago, and he doesn't know much either. Said he thought he'd taken care of the matter last week. Then late last night the same reporter called, telling him what he's got and does Lumpkin have anything to add to it? Lumpkin said he tried stalling, asking for time to confirm the information, and could the reporter wait a day before running with it. But the guy was adamant. Said his source was unimpeachable, and he wasn't holding it up."

"Did he mention his source?" I asked, praying it wasn't Carol.

Scully shook his head. "He tried getting it out of him. The only thing he said was if Lumpkin had something to add he'd include it."

My stomach turned. I saw the entire case going down the toilet.

"What about your friend, you think she knows anything?" Scully asked.

I felt my face warm under his gaze. "I tried reaching her, but she's out of town till Friday," I said, and left it at that. "How many outside our organization you figure are in the loop on the case?"

Scully heaved a sigh. "Hell, I don't know. I've been keeping the Vice Chief informed. No tellin' who besides the CNO he's brought in. Could be the whole friggin' E-Ring."

I thought of my discussions with Carol and figured that between Scully and me, the odds favored most of the Navy staff.

"So what do we do now, Chief?"

"Nothing."

"Nothing?"

Tapping the newspaper with his finger, he explained, "They've pulled the rug out from under us. I expect the case will soon be out of our hands, if it isn't already."

I wanted to say we never really owned it. Instead, I said, "It's over, just like that?"

"'Fraid so."

"What about the press? What do we tell them?"

He waved that away. "Not our problem. Lumpkin will deal with them."

I didn't want it to end, not this way, and I countered, "And Espy, the guy who put Resnick in the tower, what happens to him?"

"Can you prove it?"

"No," I admitted, shifting in my chair.

For the first time, Scully offered a slight grin. "If it's any consolation, his time in this town is over, and probably with the Navy, too."

I thought of Espy accusing me of sullying his name, and felt some satisfaction that it had been. But by whom and to what end?

* * *

It wasn't until Friday before I began getting some answers. When I phoned this time, Carol was in. And while she didn't sound overly enthused, neither was she hostile.

"Hi," I said. "I know you said not to call, but I need to see you."

"This is really a bad time. I've been out of town and have a lot of catching up."

"You saw the *Post* story?" When she said she had, I said, "It's important that we talk." There was a silence that had me asking, "You there?"

"I'm here. Look, Jerzy, I'm not sure that's a good idea right now."

"This isn't about us," I said before she said something I didn't want to hear. "Well, I guess it is in a way, but that isn't why I have to see you. This Resnick case has been turned on its ear and I need answers. Something out of the ordinary happened, and I'm in the middle of it. I need to know what's going on, and why and how I got pulled into it. And," I added in a softer tone, "if you'll tell me, I'd like to know about us. Last Saturday I was on cloud nine, and now I don't know where I stand with you." I must have sounded desperate, because her manner changed.

"Okay," she said. Then, after an agonizing pause, she said, "Can you come by tonight, around ten?"

"Try to stop me," I said, and delighted in hearing her laugh.

Nineteen

I stopped at a florist on the way home and stood looking through the window. The flowers had been welcomed before, why not again? Yet, they seemed more
a bribe now than a token of affection. What to do? I
was turning away when I glimpsed a miniature potted
cactus.

I left the house at nine thirty, the cactus buckled
into the seat beside me. While heading south through
Old Town my thoughts altered between Espy's role in
the Resnick case and how best to patch things up with
Carol.

I was waiting for a break in traffic, halfway into my
turn toward the river. Directly ahead, set squarely in
the intersection atop an eight-foot granite base, stood
the town's Civil War memorial, a life-size bronze
Confederate soldier gazing south, his arms folded
defiantly across his chest. Like most drivers, I barely
noticed it anymore, and simply steered around it,
which I was about to do when I glanced up and realized the driver behind me wasn't going to stop.

In the next instant I was propelled into the granite base and, like a doll in a cement mixer, I hit the steering wheel and was thrown back against my seat with equal force, at which point the air bag exploded and I blacked out.

When I opened my eyes the world was hazy, as if I were peering through gauze. A shadowy figure beside me was pounding my door and shouting, "Get outta there!"

Yes, I thought, that's what I need to do, but I was pinned between the steering wheel and my twisted seat, held there by a seatbelt that wouldn't unlock. Not one to give up, especially when my life's at stake, I struggled to undo myself while praying the distant sirens would arrive before the gas fumes I smelled ignited.

Thankfully they did, and soon someone popped my window, and I sucked in the welcome rush of fresh air. From over my shoulder a voice asked if I was all right, and I replied, "I think so, but I can't see. Everything's a blur."

"Stand clear!" he yelled, and in the next instant my door was torn away and I was being cut loose and fitted with a neck brace. Strong hands eased me out and onto a gurney, where I repeated my concern about not being able to see. Moments later an EMT was flushing my eyes with water and explaining how blood from my head cuts had caked the powder from the air bag.

"How's that?" she asked, patting my face dry.

"Much better," I said, blinking her into focus while she went on about head wounds bleeding excessively because of the many veins there, and often looking more severe than they actually are. It was information that would have been interesting another time.

Once in the ambulance, I was hooked up to a heart monitor and fitted with oxygen tubes. Between queries about how I felt and questions about my medical history I inquired about the other driver. "Is he okay?"

"We don't know," the attendant replied. "It was a hit-and-run."

Later, in the emergency room—after the x-rays and an MRI scan—I told the officer who showed up to take my statement to phone Barone.

Somewhere around midnight I felt a gentle hand on my shoulder rocking me awake. It was Barone.

"Hiya," he said. "You're getting to be a fulltime pain in the ass." He said it with enough of a smile to let me know he didn't mean it. "How ya feeling?"

"Like shit. That's the good news. Tomorrow, they say, I'll feel worse."

He nodded. "Count on it. From what I hear you're lucky to be alive. Had he been going faster you'd be a permanent part of that monument." Then, shaking his head, he said, "Never understood why they planted that thing there in the first place. Probably making a statement." Then, "I'm guessing since you contacted me you figure it wasn't an accident."

My mouth was dry, and I asked for water. After sipping some, I said, "Hit-and-run tells me it could be connected to——"

"Your guy who made the papers this week?" he said, finishing my thought. "Or maybe that Joe fella from the nursing home?"

"Yeah," I said shifting my body, and wincing at the pain arching across my shoulders. "Looks like I won't have to wait till tomorrow." He offered to call a nurse, and I said it wasn't necessary. "At first I thought it might've been someone who panicked and fled—some jerk on a cell phone, or a drunk."

"And now you're thinking you were followed?" Barone asked.

I gave a weak nod. "I remember there wasn't much traffic when I left the parkway at the top of Old Town. He was hanging back, shifting lanes when I did."

"Probably waiting to see where you parked."

"So he could attack me when I returned."

"But changed his mind when you stopped at the intersection. The statue there in front of you. Saw a chance and grabbed it."

"Then takes off."

"Likely picked you up at your home."

I considered that, and said, "I don't recall seeing anyone when I left."

"Probably had other things on your mind."

"Whatya mean?"

Barone grinned. "A late date?"

"What makes you say that?" I asked, thinking I should call Carol. Let her know what happened.

He held up the accident report. "Doesn't take a detective. Sports jacket, tie, clean shaven and," he said, sniffing, "enough cologne to float a battleship. The only thing I can't figure out is the cactus."

"It isn't worth explaining," I said. "Any witnesses?"

"Several. Gave us a make on the vehicle and a partial license number—a dark green Ford pickup with West Virginia tags. A couple waiting to cross described the driver as a lone white male. Another witness said he continued south. Didn't stop or slow down, just kept going."

"Doesn't sound like something Espy would drive," I said. "I see him in a Porsche or a Jag."

"We'll know more in the morning," he said. "I expect you'll be here a day or two. If not, I know where to find you."

Soon after he left they transferred me to a room upstairs. By then I was exhausted and ready for sleep, but they kept waking me throughout the night checking my vitals.

Later that morning, around nine, I phoned Theo and told him what had happened and asked that he inform Scully. When I mentioned what Barone had said about the pickup with West Virginia tags, he stopped me.

"West Virginia!" he cried.

"What about it?"

"Your old cases. One involved a San Diego-based boatswain, name of Bobby Lee Adair."

"I remember," I said. "He'd been sexually abusing his step-daughter, a shy young thing." It was impossible to forget those cases, especially when I was the sole savior for so many defenseless victims. "She came forward after his ship deployed. I picked him up in Pearl Harbor and brought him back. A piece of human garbage. Made me want to administer some frontier justice before turning him in. As I recall, he pled and got a reduced sentence."

"That's him," Theo said. "And do you also recall he was from Keyser, West Virginia?"

"Better contact Detective Barone," I said.

My phone rang about two hours later. It was Barone. "Feelin' better?" he asked.

"It's like they said, stiff and sore, but otherwise okay. I haven't seen the doc yet, but I expect he'll want me to take it easy for a few days. But enough about me. You heard from Theo?" And when he said he had, I asked, "Anything new?"

"Fairfax PD found the pickup a mile south of town, at the Belle Haven Marina. Left front tire shredded. No sign of the driver."

"Did you get a hit on the owner?" I asked.

"Asshole removed the tags, but we traced him through the VIN. Vehicle belongs to a Jackson Turner out of Keyser, West Virginia. The town matches what your colleague told us, but not the name. You remember a Jackson Turner involved with that Adair case?"

I thought hard but drew a blank. "The name doesn't register. I'll have Theo search the case file and get back to you. Meanwhile, you may want to check with the local sheriff, see if there's a connection to Adair."

"Don't know what we'd do without you NCIS boys," he said. "I already placed the call."

"Just trying to help."

"Well, just try getting better," he said before hanging up.

Considering what I had been through I was feeling pretty good when they discharged me later that day. And while I dressed myself without too much trouble, I was thankful I had worn loafers because I never could have bent to tie my laces. Afterward, the nurse, a perky Filippina, came in and reminded me to get plenty of rest and take Percocet as needed. She then handed me over to a volunteer, who wheeled me to the hospital van. The day was bright and warm and I felt well enough to fly solo. But that changed. When I got home I must have turned too sharply in my seat, causing every back muscle to seize. The driver, a gracious Middle Eastern fellow, sprang to my aid, helping me as far as the front door, where he offered to assist me into bed. I thanked him, saying I was all right now that I was up and walking.

After downing a Percocet, I hobbled to the phone, eased into a chair, and checked in with Scully. His wife answered, and immediately began quizzing me. And while I appreciated her concern, she continued on longer than necessary. Finally, with the conversation growing stale, she wished me well and relinquished the phone to Scully.

"Hiya, Chief," I said with as much energy as I could muster, and then brought him up to date on what I had learned from Theo and Barone.

"So it looks like our boy Espy's clear on this one," he said.

"It would seem so. And probably the break-in here and the attempt on Sis's life," I added.

"You don't recall anyone named Turner?" And when I said no, he said, "Too bad. Doesn't matter. We'll get the bastard." I could hear his wife fussing in the background. "Sorry," he said to both of us, "Got carried away. Incidentally, what were you hoping to learn from Captain Rutter, anyway?"

"Well," I said, thinking I needed to call her next, "this business with the leak to the *Post* left me unsettled, and I wanted to see what she could tell me about it." *Plus, I fell for her, and was hoping to work things out between us.*

He wished me luck, and I almost said I'd need it.

"Meanwhile, watch your back," he said. "Turner sounds determined."

I told him I wasn't concerned, adding, "He's probably back in West Virginia by now. Besides, Barone's got his guys patrolling the neighborhood."

"That's fine, but keep alert anyway." Before hanging up, he said, "If you're thinking about coming in, forget it. Stay home and get well."

I said I intended to, and hung up. The medicine was making me drowsy. One more call, I thought, then off to bed—if I can manage the stairs—otherwise the sofa.

It was nearly five, and I figured, this being Saturday, Carol should be home from the Pentagon by now. She answered on the second ring.

"I'm not accustomed to being stood up," she said right off, and then quickly apologized when I told her what happened and what I knew about the driver and the possible connection to a previous case.

And while she sounded concerned—which I took as a good sign—she was equally pleased to learn Espy was likely off the hook for the nursing home incident.

"I'd still like to see you," I told her, "but not tonight. Maybe in a few days, when I'm feeling better."

"Sure. We'll talk then."

It took some effort to stand, and several minutes to negotiate the stairs, but I was determined to reach my bed. It wasn't till I made the final step that I remembered the fish. I hadn't fed them in two days, maybe three. "I'll make it up to you tomorrow, guys," I called, before hobbling to my room. I was craving sleep and, rather than undress, I kicked off my shoes and fell across the bed.

I'm not clear what roused me, whether it was the faint odor of gasoline or the pounding on the door, but in my semi-conscious fog I was once again trapped in my car, struggling to get out before it exploded.

The room was dark, and it wasn't till I found the lamp switch that I realized I wasn't dreaming. The odor was real as was the pounding. Thinking Turner had returned for another try, I slipped on my shoes, grabbed my revolver, and eased my way downstairs. I was ready for him this time.

TWENTY

By the time I reached the front door my eyes were tearing from the fumes. Rather than expose myself by switching on the light I angled to the window and peered out. No Turner. Instead there was an Arlington police officer holding his handkerchief to his nose. I pocketed my gun, opened the door, and stepped outside into a pool of gasoline. Before I could ask what was going on, he had my arm and was pulling me onto the lawn.

"Agent Shore?" And when I nodded, he pointed over his shoulder to his partner and the wiry man cuffed and face down across the hood of the patrol car. "That guy was about to torch your house. Another few minutes, and you would've been toast."

All I saw were his faded jeans, denim jacket and work boots, but I figured it had to be Jackson Turner, or Joe, or whatever he went by, and I started for him. The officer wisely blocked me.

"That bastard tried to kill my sister!"

"Take it easy. He's not going anywhere," he said while his partner yanked him by the collar and folded him into the rear seat.

"Just give me a minute with him," I said.

"I know how you feel," he sympathized. "But there's too many eyes around."

The car door slammed and his linebacker partner came over carrying a weathered billfold.

"Says here on his driver's license," he said, shining his flashlight on the cracked plastic sleeve, "Bobby Lee Adair of Keyser, West Virginia. That ain't the name we got earlier," he told his partner.

"Adair! The sonofabitch is out."

"What's that?" the first officer said, and I quickly explained. When we looked back at the car he was grinning at us.

Minutes later screaming fire engines filled the street, and for the second time in two days I was surrounded by flashing lights and suited men.

I soon learned Adair was determined to get me this time. In addition to the gasoline splashed across the front of my house, they found a second unopened container on the rear deck beside the kitchen door. That one the police removed as evidence, while noting, "He was going to be sure you didn't get out." They left soon afterward with Adair glaring at me.

I asked a fireman about hosing down the house and was told to do nothing until the Hazmat team arrived. And when I moved to go inside, I was deterred again.

"We can't let you inside either," he informed me.

"It's just a little gasoline," I protested.

He shook his head. "EPA rules."

"You're joking."

He shrugged. "No joke."

Curious, I asked, "How would you handle it without EPA?"

He grinned. "We'd hose down the house and let you inside."

By now, most of the neighbors were awake, and those who weren't at their windows had gathered curbside across the street. The young couple next door, having edged close enough to hear my predicament, kindly invited me inside.

It was nearly four thirty when the Hazmat team finished wiping down the house and porch with absorbent pads, which they sealed in steel barrels. As they were packing their gear and preparing to leave, I walked over and was informed I could safely enter now.

Despite their best efforts, the house still reeked of gasoline. The odor, along with images of Adair torching me, kept me tossing till dawn, which is when I hooked up my hose and sprayed the house.

I did it again around ten, and once more at noon. I was preparing to feed my fish when the doorbell rang. I had been carrying my gun all morning—you might say I was paranoid—and I unholstered it. I knew it wasn't Adair, and not knowing who else besides Turner was working with him, I edged to the window and peered out. It was Barone, no doubt coming to tell me what he had learned about the pair.

"Geez," he said shaking his head as he entered. "How do you stand it?"

I sniffed and said, "It's hardly noticeable."

"You got a problem, my friend."

"Might explain why the coffee lacked taste," I said. "You want a cup?"

He shook his head and reached into his jacket for his cigar stub. Then, looking around, returned it. "Well, I don't know if you believe in Karma, but this Adair case nearly came around and bit you square in the ass."

"I'm sure you've had a few like it," I said. He didn't respond, but I could tell I hit a nerve. "So what's the story?"

"According to the Keyser sheriff, Jackson Turner, the owner of the vehicle, is Bobby Lee Adair's brother-in-law. Adair was released from a halfway house three months ago and headed back to Keyser, where he hooked up with his wife, who'd been living with the Turners. Both men are employed by CSX at the rail yard there. Turner full-time and Adair a provisional, so long as he keeps his nose clean."

"And their second job's hunting me." I said.

Barone shook his head. "Doesn't look that way. Adair seems to be acting alone. From what the sheriff says, this Turner's a devoted family man—upstanding citizen, church-goer, never been in trouble. Looks like Adair used Turner's truck without telling him what he intended. It's probably like we said. He was tailing you and likely saw an opportunity and took it. Nevertheless we're checking out Turner's whereabouts the nights the candy was left at the nursing home and your place was broken into to be sure it wasn't him."

"And, Adair? What's he got to say?"

"Not a word, except he wants a lawyer."

"No doubt blames me for his conviction."

Barone shrugged. "These morons wanna blame everyone but themselves for their troubles. Lucky most don't have half a brain, and we stop 'em before they do any real harm. Unfortunately, a few like your friend Adair get lucky and succeed. This one wasn't going to quit till he got you."

"And he would have if it wasn't for you and your men. I owe you."

"We'll talk about that later."

I thought about Sis, and asked "Think you'll be able to tie him to the nursing home?" Then, knowing what was coming, I said, "You're going to need someone to ID him, place him there."

"Yep," he said, pulling out Adair's booking photo. "We'll talk to the staff. See if anyone recognizes him. Meanwhile, you might want to show this to your sister."

I studied Adair's sour expression. "She won't be a credible witness."

"I know. Still, it's one more arrow in our quiver if she IDs him."

"I'll try," I said. "You sure you don't want coffee, or something stronger?"

"No, thanks," he said looking around. "Nice place you got here. Very comfortable."

"It's the positive chi."

"The what?"

I considered enlightening him, but decided against it. "Nothing, really."

He looked at me and squinted.

When we reached the door, he sniffed again and said, "Doesn't smell so bad after a while. Still, you oughta get away a few days till this shit clears, or you won't be able to taste anything."

"I just might."

"I'll be talking to you," he said from over his shoulder. He took only a few steps before retrieving his cigar stub and shoving it in his mouth.

TWENTY-ONE

Things were much improved by Tuesday. I was getting around without the Percocet, and after several more hosings the gasoline odor was finally gone. It was time, I decided, to call Carol. I reached her at work, and when I suggested we get together, she said, "You mean tonight?"

Her response threw me, and I asked, "Not a good time?"

There was a pause that left me wondering whether she wanted to see me at all. "I guess it'll be okay," she said. "I can swing by on the way home sometime after nine, if that's convenient."

I assured her it was, and gave her the address. At eight thirty I called for Chinese take-out and chilled a bottle of Chardonnay. Then, under the cover of darkness, I liberated a few of my neighbor's daffodils and set them out in a vase.

By nine I had changed clothes twice before finally opting for a pair of chinos and a classic blue button-down shirt. Meanwhile, I'd been preparing what I intended to say about the *Post* leak and the thorny issue of our relationship. And while I was clear about the leak, I hadn't come close to resolving the other issue. Where, I wondered, was my positive chi?

The food had cooled when she finally arrived near ten. And, like Barone, she wrinkled her nose. "Whew," she said walking quickly past me. "How do you stand it?"

So much for the welcome kiss. "It should be gone by tomorrow," I said, leading her back to the kitchen, where I hoped the air was fresher. On the way, I told her of Adair's attempt at roasting me, and why, and was pleased to see her manner soften.

Reaching out, she touched my bruised face, and said, "You've had a rough time."

I was still looking for that kiss, but it didn't come. Instead, she said she was famished and we settled in to eat, and didn't get around to discussing the case until afterward. By then, we had moved into the living room, the half empty wine bottle on the table between us. She had been quiet throughout dinner, and now she was sitting stiffly across from me, her body language suggesting she didn't want to be here.

As I refilled our glasses I said, "My boss informed me the Resnick case is over and I should move on."

"He's right." She said it in a way that had me thinking she had already done so.

"The problem is I can't just walk away from it."

She sipped her wine and studied her glass. "I guess you must feel used."

"Like a doormat."

"That's too bad," she said without much sympathy.

"The problem is too many holes."

"And you'd like me to fill them in."

"That's what I was hoping."

"It's complicated," she said, setting down her glass.

"Such things usually are."

"You want my advice, Jerzy, listen to your boss and let go. You're not going to change anything."

"That's not my nature, to let go."

"Which, I suppose, is why you're good at what you do."

"And which is probably why I got dragged into this case," I said, and watched her stiffen.

"I didn't have anything to do with that."

"I'm not saying you did. But someone in the E-Ring wanted this case handled at the headquarters level, where they could monitor and control it, rather than at the academy where it belonged."

She licked her lips, and said, "You're making things difficult."

"Another character flaw," I said. "That aside, let's be honest. This charade was never about ferreting out Jeff Resnick's killer, if ever there was one, was it? The leak to the newspaper pretty much confirmed that NCIS—for whatever reason—was brought in to destroy Espy. To give the accusation the necessary credibility. Will you at least concede that much?"

"I'd like to hear more first."

"All right. I also believe the business about Espy being a Green Bowler was a ruse. It couldn't be as Admiral Poff related it."

She frowned, and asked, "What business?"

"CNO's assertion that Captain Briggs, the former commandant, and Espy were Green Bowlers, and used their affiliation to cover up Espy's connection to Resnick."

"I don't understand."

I doubted that, but withheld saying so. "It was important to strengthen the case against Espy that I buy into the idea he was a Bowler. But first I had to know about the cover-up, which is where your friend the Marine colonel came in; telling me that Espy had initiated the banner prank and later instructed him and the others to keep mum about it, while assuring them he'd handle the investigation. So, when Poff told me about the Green Bowlers and CNO's disclosure that Briggs was one, it followed that Espy had to be one too. How else could he have ensured that he and his classmates would be excluded from the investigation?"

"Which only proves Ron is a Green Bowler," she argued.

I shook my head. "Briggs may've been a Bowler, but not Espy, not based on what I've learned of the organization. The CNO would have to be one to know about Briggs. And, if the CNO is a Bowler, he wouldn't be passing that info on to Poff, who isn't one. Nor would he have thrown Espy under the bus if he were a fellow member. It doesn't work that way."

For the first time she smiled. "You're good."

"There's more," I said, enjoying the compliment. "I'm willing to bet that mister-fourth-generation-Annapolis Ted Benson is a Green Bowler, as well."

She was leaning forward now. "On what basis?"

"He praised Espy too much in an effort to disguise the poison."

"What poison?"

"Letting me know Espy wasn't someone you wanted to piss off."

She shook her head. "Ted was never subtle."

"It worked," I said. "That seemingly casual remark, along with the colonel's comments, kept the investigation focused on Espy." I poured the remaining wine into our glasses, sat back, and said, "Which is why I believe the colonel is also a Bowler."

"I see where this is going," she said.

"Do the Green Bowlers allow women in?" I asked.

She shifted slightly. "Don't be coy, Jerzy. It isn't becoming. Say it. You believe I'm a Green Bowler, as well."

"It would seem so under the circumstances," I said, hoping for a denial.

She had taken up her glass, and was smiling into it. "I hate to disappoint you," she said looking up, "but you've got it wrong."

"You're not a Bowler?"

"No, and neither is the colonel or Ted." To my surprise, she said, "You're also wrong about Ron. He is a Green Bowler."

I shook my head. "How would you know if you aren't one? Unless…"

"…unless it was pillow talk?" she said without hiding her displeasure. "It has nothing to do with that."

I was about to apologize, when her expression softened. "Poor Jerzy. I'm afraid we've put you through the wringer." In the next instant she was beside me and we were kissing. How I yearned for those kisses, to hold her and taste her sweet breath again. I said I missed her and hoped she felt the same. She assured me she did, adding how she had wanted to come to me earlier. And when I asked why she hadn't, she said she was frightened at the intensity of her feelings after our night together. I was jubilant.

Well, that's how I wished it happened but, of course, it didn't. Not even close. Carol never left her chair. Instead, she remained there studying me and strumming her fingers on the arm. Finally, her hand fell still and she said, "I'm going to breach a confidence and tell you something few people know, and which you probably won't believe. Naturally, I prefer you not share it." Then, taking a breath, she said, "You're in the right church, but the wrong pew."

"Care to clarify?" I said.

"You're right about discrediting Ron with the news leak. That was the intent from the beginning."

"So, Lumpkin's in this, too."

She shook her head. "He knows nothing of this. He and the Chinfo team are as innocent as you. The leak originated elsewhere. Obviously, I won't tell you where."

My mind was racing now. "It doesn't make sense. If Espy's a Green Bowler, as you say, then CNO's one too. Why would he throw a fellow Bowler under the bus?"

"That's where you're in the wrong pew," she said, before relating an astonishing tale dating back to the early nineteenth century, soon after Commodore Stephen Decatur, the naval hero credited with defeating the Barbary Pirates, had been killed in a duel with Captain James Barron in nearby Bladensburg, Maryland.

"You're familiar with the Decatur House in Lafayette Square, across from the White House?" she asked.

I said I was, but had never been inside.

"It became a monument soon after his death. And within its walls a society was formed, which became a formidable force within naval circles. Its purpose, to maintain the Navy's prestige and political strength by perpetuating the memory of its most famous hero. The group, known only to its members, was the Decatur Party." Smiling proudly, she added, "It was led by a woman. Decatur's fiery widow, Susan."

"And this is tied to Espy how?"

She was still smiling when she said, "A century later, members of the Decatur Party formed a second secret society."

"The Green Bowlers!"

She finished her wine and, with an amused expression, said, "It gets better. The Green Bowlers had no knowledge of the Decatur Party. The goal," she explained, "was to create an outer circle whose members believe they are a primary force for change, when in reality they act on behalf of the far more secret inner circle. Naturally, no one among the Green Bowlers may join the ranks of the Decaturs, but select members of the Decaturs are Green Bowlers."

"So, for you to know Espy's a Green Bowler and not be one yourself means you're a Decatur."

She didn't reply directly. Instead, she said, "The organization has worn many faces over the years."

I was wondering how many of those faces I had encountered, when she started in about the need for a strong navy. "Just a second," I said. "You still haven't told me why Espy was targeted."

Her expression suggested the reason was obvious. If so, I hadn't grasped it.

"I'm getting to that," she said. "The force transformation initiative is in the process of altering the size and mission of our Navy." And when I mentioned the Cold War being over and new threats posed by rogue states and insurgent groups, she waved me off. "Wrong! That's what this misguided president and his advisors want us to believe, so they can justify replacing our large deck platforms with smaller inferior ones, which they intend scattering around the globe in distant ports. It's a seditious plot intended to weaken our maritime capability and squander our limited assets."

"And Espy failed to understand this?"

"Ron was placed in that office to impede their efforts, but at some point he forgot what color his uniform is. He and his boss were pressing too hard, making deals with Congress that undercut essential shipbuilding programs to compensate for new weapons systems with no strategic value."

"And discrediting Espy remedies that?"

"It's one step in the process."

"He's that important?"

"Removing him will have an impact," she assured me. "In fact, it already has," she said without pleasure.

I was about to ask how, but knew she wouldn't tell me. She was in a league I wasn't qualified to play in. I also realized she had nothing to fear by telling me of the Decatur-Green Bowler cabal, since I had no way of corroborating it. Still, I wondered why disclose it to me, an outsider? And then it struck me. She did indeed care for Espy, and blowing him out of the water, as they had, was distasteful and counter to her feelings for him. And, since she couldn't share that sentiment with her confederates without calling her own loyalty into question, this was her one chance to vent.

"And you're okay with that?" I asked.

"It was the most expeditious way of dealing with the situation," she said without feeling. "Well?" she said when I had fallen quiet.

"I was recalling something from a biography of the Spanish dictator Francisco Franco. When one of his generals was asked about the atrocities being committed during the civil war, he replied, 'We have to eliminate without scruples or hesitation all those who do not think as we do.'"

"I'll remember that," she said, nodding her approval.

"Will you answer this for me? Was Espy complicit in Resnick's death?"

"He sent Jeff into the tower. I don't know if he accompanied him. I don't think so. Nor do I believe he intended Jeff harm. I can tell you he didn't grieve over his death. As I told you before, he was jealous of our friendship."

"But jealousy doesn't explain sending Resnick to the tower. What would Espy have gained had he completed the task?"

"I suspect he had someone waiting to catch Jeff as he slipped back into Bancroft, which was a serious offense."

What a conniving bastard."

"I know," is all she said.

Moving on, I said, "You realize your letter caused a great deal of pain to the Resnicks."

She shook her head. "That's regrettable, but timing was critical. Action had to be taken before certain commitments were forged on the Hill."

"I'm having difficulty with that," I said. "I met with the Resnicks, and the wife is a fragile lady. This entire episode has affected her terribly."

"Since you're fond of historical quotes, do you recall General William Tecumseh Sherman's famous quote?" And when I shrugged, she said "'War is cruelty. You cannot refine it.' We did what we had to do."

"Did it for whom?" I asked.

Squaring her shoulders, she said, "When I commanded a destroyer in the Pacific, we made our first foreign port call to Maizuru, a picturesque town in western Japan, its harbor sheltered by verdant hills. The mayor and several local dignitaries were gathered on the pier as we entered port. I was on the wing of the bridge." Her voice seemed to draw power from itself as she spoke. "It was an exhilarating sight, one I shall long remember, but not as exhilarating as looking up and seeing my country's flag flying from the mast of my ship. I will never forget that day. My skin tingled with pride as I felt the power of my country surging through my veins. So, to answer your question, we did it for America. To keep her strong. I hope you understand that." Then, without warning, she stood. "It's late. I must go."

"Wait!" I said, jumping up to meet her. She couldn't leave without my asking, "What about us?"

She looked at me with genuine surprise. "What about us?"

I swallowed hard. "What I mean is… Is there an us?"

She sighed. "You're a sweet man, Jerzy, but I thought you figured that out."

"Figured what out?"

"That it wasn't going anywhere. That my career doesn't permit distractions. That there's no room for anyone in my life, certainly not now."

I thought, how do you counter that? But I tried. "What about our night together?"

Her eyes washed over me. "It was lovely, but you're making too much of it."

"Too much? How's that possible?"

"I'm not sure what you're looking for, but you won't find it here," she said.

We were in the center of the room, much as we had been at her place not two weeks earlier, but the magic was gone. The roller coaster had stopped. The ride was over.

After an awkward silence, I forced a smile and said, "So, I guess this means you won't be spending the night."

She laughed. "I do like that about you, Jerzy Shore, your perseverance." When we reached the door, she turned and said, "A note of caution. Be careful. You fall in love too easily."

I stood at the curb long after she drove away, thinking she might return. When she didn't, I went inside and fed the fish.

Acknowledgements

I am deeply grateful to retired Special Agents Pete Hughes, NCIS Cold Case Homicide Unit, and John Tigmo, NCIS Forensic Consultant Unit, for their assistance in helping me understand the nuances of their trade. I am also indebted to the members of my writers group for their positive feedback and constructive criticism. Specifically, I wish to thank Carolin Crabbe, Valery Garrett, Cynthia Gayton, Clyde Linsley, Nina Holachek, Adelaida Lucenda de Lower, John Mallon, Michael Williams, Johanna Willner, and Mary Wuest whose comments and dedication to the writing craft helped shape Jerzy Shore into a credible character. I would also like to thank Captain Bob Berkeley, JAG, USN (Ret.), NYFD Battalion Chief Bill Koehler (Ret.), and former NCIS Special Agent Joe Riccio for their kind assistance. And a special note of thanks to Ed Jaffee, whose keen eyes, proofreading skills, and quick wit have once again proven invaluable.

About The Author

George Vercessi is a retired U.S. Navy captain residing in Virginia with his wife, Barbara. He is currently involved in several writing projects, including a second novel featuring Jerzy Shore, and another centering on Charlie Paradise, the nonconforming bail bondsman whose mobile office once served as a lunch wagon, and who occasionally finds himself in need of bail.